THE CRIME O

The Crime of Colours

ANDREW BRANDON

KINGSWAY PUBLICATIONS
EASTBOURNE

First published 1993

ISBN 0 85476 3430

Produced by Bookprint Creative Services
P.O. Box 827, BN23 6NX, England for
KINGSWAY PUBLICATIONS LTD
Lottbridge Drove, Eastbourne, E Sussex BN23 6NT
Printed in Great Britain by Clays Ltd, St Ives PLC
Typeset by J&L Composition Ltd, Filey, North Yorkshire

Contents

1

The Dream

Joanna slept, the lovely oval of her face glistening in the moonlight. Her room was tidy and ordered: books lined shelves in neat formations; tomorrow's clothes lay pressed and folded on a stiff-backed chair; a poster of a whale hung on the wall above her bed; and on her desk top her computer monitor shimmered in the glow of a nearby street lamp.

Joanna tossed, a sudden, unexpected motion that spilled her curls across the pillow. The dream came to her, calling, beckoning: the sharp, salt twang of the sea; the feel of the sand beneath her feet and the wind on her upturned face; the surf exploding on the beach with the boom, boom of artillery fire. A slender wooden pier braved the fury of the waves and drove into the sea for a short distance; and standing on its tip, a tall, cloaked figure.

Dawn! The sun climbed above the rim of the sea and balanced on the tight-rope of the horizon. In its centre stood the man, silhouetted like a dark splinter in its burning eye. The picture blazed in Joanna's imagination: the sun turning the sea into a storm of fire, into the lake of hell itself, and the stranger riding the storm like a demon king.

'We send you into exile, Dimrat!' The speaker was hidden from Joanna's view by an outcrop of rock, but his voice was keen and strong, silencing the clamour of the surf like a judge's gavel. 'We send you to the icelands of the north. From this day forth you will be an outcast. The doors of the world will be shut against you!'

On the pier, the stranger raised a fist and snarled, his lean face twisted in rage and loathing. 'I curse you sun,' he rasped, his voice screeching above the thunder of the waves. 'I curse all beauty and song, all laughter and colour. I summon the . . .'

His speech was interrupted by a joyful cry: 'The dolphins! The dolphins are coming!' The cry was immediately repeated by a chorus of excited voices: 'The dolphins! The dolphins!' Bearing down on Dimrat from the heart of the ocean was a school of dolphins. Joanna was stunned by their grace and wild majesty. As they sped towards the pier, the sun caught them, transforming their lithe bodies into rainbows of dancing light.

As they sang, the dolphins leaped to and fro across the prow of a tiny boat moored to the tip of the pier, weaving ropes of plaited kelp around its gilded figurehead. Dimrat sat in the bow, tall and imposing, a sinister intrusion into the joy and innocence of those creatures.

'Go into exile!' commanded the voice. The dolphins, obedient to this command, erupted into life. Northward they sped, towing the boat with such violence that a foaming wave lifted the prow and scattered spray over Dimrat. He turned, aware at last of the presence of Joanna, and trapped her with his eyes. His eyes were the last sequence of the dream, the moment of extreme terror that drove her from sleep into trembling wakefulness.

Joanna's room was tidy and ordered but no longer safe. She sat up in bed, pushed a tangle of curls from her eyes and reached for her lamp switch. Light swamped the room, drowned the shadows, oozed into dark corners. She swung her legs from bed to

8

floor in one movement, paused for a moment, and then walked unsteadily to her desk. Opening her diary, she wrote: 'The dream has come again. I wish it would go away. What does it mean? Who is Dimrat? What is his crime? I'm afraid to sleep, and when I awake I cannot forget the venom spurting from his eyes.'

Beneath Joanna's window, a stranger stood and watched, his skin a rich purple black, his eyes pools of ancient light. The clothes he wore were shabby and his shoes were chafed through long acquaintance with the road, but power and goodness radiated from him like waves of light. He looked up at the window, nodded his head in evident satisfaction and then vanished, the darkness quivering like a curtain behind him.

The Captain had made his choice.

2

The Airship

The airship hung in the night like a vast shadow, blotting out the pale moon and the flickering neon of the stars. Joanna opened her window and leaned out, shivering in the autumn chill. Beneath the huge belly of the ship, suspended by a system of girders and cables, were the living quarters and navigational deck. No lights twinkled in the cabin windows and the engine was silent. The airship seemed as empty as the sky that held it.

Joanna studied the airship. A rope ladder swung from the underside of the ship to the street below her window. 'It must belong to a company . . . probably use it for advertising . . . must have broken loose from its moorings,' she reasoned. The more Joanna thought about the airship, however, the greater became her desire to climb the ladder. 'I could have one brief look, just one,' she thought, 'and then I'll wake Dad and Mum and we'll inform the police.' A more dramatic thought occurred to her, sending a sudden thrill of excitement through her body: 'The airship may have been hijacked by terrorists . . . the passengers are hostages.'

Joanna imagined herself standing before the Queen to receive a medal for gallantry. The thought came so vividly that she could hear the Queen's voice, the elastic vowels stretching each word, the upper-class accent: 'It gives me great pleasure, Joanna Bradley, to award you this medal for your gallantry in assisting the police with the arrest of the airship hijackers. Your bravery is an example to the youth of Britain.'

Joanna's brow puckered in a frown of embarrassment. 'That's kids' stuff,' she told herself, but the pull of the airship grew stronger.

Joanna was an intelligent girl, as the school certificates on her walls confirmed, but she was also tough and independent. Life in Brixton had forged her character and given it a depth and maturity unusual in a girl of sixteen. She loved the raw energy of the streets, the cocktail of races, and above all the acceptance people gave her as the daughter of mixed-race parents. But Brixton did not own her. Joanna was a loner, a wild, poetic girl, with dreams as big as the world. She matched herself against the airship's ladder and was certain that she could master it. It was not courage that drove her to climb, but curiosity, the determination to plunder the secrets of that huge, silent airship.

Slipping out of her pyjamas, Joanna pulled on her tee-shirt and jeans, tied the laces of her trainers and snuggled into the warmth of her quilted jacket, a sure protection against the chill of an October night. Opening the door of her parents' room, she slid inside, her eyes adjusting to the half-light.

Her parents lay clutched together in an untidy tangle of legs and arms. Joanna felt a rush of tenderness. Sleep had stolen their dignity and turned them into children. Her mother's skin appeared even blacker in the moonlight, contrasting with the pallor of her father's face and shoulders. Her father's hair was untidy and his mouth hung open in a gape of astonishment. His rough, irregular snores punctuated the stillness of the room, lending a strong bass support to her mother's calypso breathing. 'Dad doesn't do anything quietly,' she thought, resisting the temptation to fill his mouth with the sock that he had abandoned on the bedside table. Joanna chuckled to herself, imagining her mother's comments in the morning: 'Can't you even leave your clothes in a tidy pile, man? You're more trouble than a child!'

She caught her reflection in the wardrobe mirror and admired herself briefly: a tall, gangling girl with dark eyes, high cheekbones, wide, tender lips and olive skin. Her eyes unfocused and she saw beyond her immediate reflection. The airship beckoned her, a ship of mystery afloat on a midnight sea. Turning for one final look at her parents, she whispered goodbye and sped from the house to the street below.

The front door clicked shut behind her.

3

The Face of Dimrat

Joanna climbed unsteadily, the rope ladder lurching and writhing beneath her with every movement of her body and flurry of wind. Studied from her window, the airship had seemed only a few metres away, but its vast size had deceived her. Shrunk by the distance to a magical toyland, the jumbled roofs and roads of suburban London receded beneath her. The city slept, but she could still hear the occasional throb of a car engine and see headlights cutting through the darkness like tracer fire. The ladder was so fragile that she felt she was not climbing at all, but floating above the dreaming city.

London lay below her, and above her, drawing ever closer, was the airship, huge and mysterious, swallowing up the stars.

Joanna was afraid. As she climbed higher, she no longer had the courage to look down. The city, so radiant in its jewellery of twinkling lights, cried out to her: 'Jump!' She felt it pulling at her feet, tearing at her fingers, dragging her down. 'No! No!' she protested, and attacked the ladder with renewed determination.

The wind which only moments before had blown in light flurries, changed direction and drove in upon Joanna with hideous force. The ladder streaked backwards and forwards; the ropes whined and hissed. Joanna's feet were torn from the rungs. Dangling by her hands, she looped the loop, somersaulted and swivelled like a trapeze acrobat in a circus.

As quickly as it came, the wind subsided. Joanna swung by her hands, her breath coming in painful, rasping sobs. For a few seconds she dangled help-lessly, and then her feet found the rung beneath her. She laughed, a short hysterical laugh, and then was overwhelmed by thankfulness. She was alive—aching, terrified, but alive.

The wind had driven a dark cloud between Joanna and the airship. As she fought against her panic, the cloud began to change shape, imperceptibly at first and then with greater purpose, until an enormous face was imposed upon the darkness of the night. The eyes were terrible: unblinking, malignant, flecked with yellow—the eyes of the natural predator. They looked upon Joanna scornfully. The lips were twisted in a cruel imitation of a smile.

'What have we here? A girl who thinks she can save an airship!' The voice was little more than a whisper, but it contained such an insinuation of evil that Joanna felt instantly defiled.

Joanna met his eyes. 'Dimrat!' she cried, spitting his name from her lips like poison. The face that hovered over her was the face in her dream. His presence sent a sudden chill of premonition through her body.

'Yes, it's me, but this time you're not dreaming. Go back. Climb down the ladder. Go home. Return to your tidy little room. Forget that you've ever seen this airship. Refuse and I will be waiting for you. You cannot escape me.'

'Why? Why don't you want me to visit the airship?' Joanna watched Dimrat's face carefully and noticed a flicker of uncertainty in his eyes; only a flicker, but it gave her hope. 'Why?' she insisted.

Dimrat parried her question with a smile, but his eyes were cold and humourless. 'Because if you go any further,' he whispered. 'I'll kill you. Now or later—it's all the same to me—you'll die, I promise you.'

The words were said with such an evil certainty

that Joanna never doubted he meant them. Dimrat laughed, and as he did so, the clouds parted and a huge hand stretched out towards her, the fingers hooked like talons.

Dimrat laughed again, a spiteful, jeering laugh.

Joanna screamed. The sound detonated deep inside her, exploding from her lips in a wail of sheer terror. The giant fingers reached for her, ready to snatch her from the ladder and toss her to the streets below. Escape was futile, but Joanna tried all the same. She hauled herself up the ladder with a desperate energy, sobbing as she climbed. 'Don't do it!' she pleaded. 'Let me go . . . Please!'

But Dimrat ignored her. He was enjoying himself immensely. He found the terror of his victims entertaining. This sobbing, terrified girl was pleading for her life. 'Well, let her continue,' he thought, 'until I tire of her.' He touched her shoulders with his fingertips, just a gentle caress, but enough to make her shriek more wildly. 'Why do they always try to escape, to live for that little bit longer?' he wondered. 'I'm glad they do. It makes the game more exciting. How tedious life would be if they accepted death with resignation!'

Dimrat paused, his hand held delicately above the neck of the terrified girl, savouring her suffering like the bouquet of the finest wine. 'So much for the maker's champion!' he thought, and then grew angry. 'Sending a girl, a child, to challenge my power. This is an insult. Who does he think I am? A sentimental old fool who'll repent of his ways as soon as he's confronted by the innocence of a girl. Idiot! I'll show him what I think of his champion!' Dimrat's good humour returned. Killing was a business he relished. 'Little sparrow,' he chided, 'why do you try and fly away from me. Be still and let me crush you in my hands, break your wings and silence your frightened chirruping. Ahh, death is so poetic!'

A sudden wild cry startled him. He withdrew his hand and looked about him. Nothing! The clouds obscured his vision so he swept them away with an impatient movement of his hand. Joanna looked up and cried out in wonder. An eagle plummeted towards Dimrat, its vast wings swept back, its talons outstretched like scimitars. Down it fell, a bird of prey in fighting fury, as fast and deadly as a blazing comet. The eagle hurled itself upon him with such terrifying power that the apparition of Dimrat was torn apart, vanishing into the darkness with a shriek of outrage that faded to a whisper.

Silence! Joanna closed her eyes very carefully and opened them again. 'I'm dreaming. It was a horrible dream. I imagined it all,' she whispered. She studied the space where the face had been, but there was nothing; no clouds, no outline of a face, no menacing hand, no eagle, only a majestic tiara of stars dangling on the brow of night. She resumed the climb, forcing herself upwards on limbs that trembled and shivered like young saplings.

The airship was much nearer now, filling the sky above her. Joanna ran her eyes along its length. 'It must be the size of two football fields,' she thought. The vast girders of the airship were etched on its skin like the ribs of a dinosaur. Beneath it hung the car, a massive ornamental structure decorated with carvings and colourful murals. 'It's fantastic,' she said aloud, and then corrected herself. 'No, not fantastic— magnificent, like an old cinema or theatre. But where are the crew? Where are the passengers?' The frail, human sound of her voice was strangely comforting.

The airship waited, floating silently on the wind like a ghost ship.

Joanna climbed the last few metres of the ladder very slowly. She looked down one last time in the hope of identifying her home, but felt so dizzy that she had to look away. Ever since the eagle had

15

destroyed the apparition of Dimrat, her fear had become more manageable. It was still there—a cold presence skulking in her guts—but somehow less intense, less powerful. 'Thank you, great eagle,' she whispered. 'You're probably only a dream, but thank you all the same.' As she spoke, a shadow skimmed the surface of the stars and quelled the moonlight with its soaring wings.

At last Joanna reached her goal. The way into the airship lay open before her. It was too late to turn back. 'If it's deserted,' she thought, 'I'll be rescued as soon as the airship is discovered. The police are bound to see it and come by helicopter to investigate. And anyway, anything's better than having to climb down that ladder, even spending the night in an empty airship.' She refused to allow herself to think of other alternatives. The idea of rescuing the crew and passengers from hijackers was no longer attractive. 'There's no point in waiting around,' she told herself bravely and heaved herself into the dark belly of the ship.

4

The Ballroom and the Banquet

Joanna threw up her hands protectively, covering her eyes. Light, as dazzling and unexpected as a photographer's flash, burst around her. As she clambered through the hatch into the airship, it came alive. One moment she was in darkness, the airship silent and unlit before her, and in the next, it was ablaze with colour. A band played in the distance. Joanna picked out the raucous wail of a saxophone and the solid beat of the drums pulsating in the floor at her feet. The airship smelled of polished wood, thick carpets and the faint yet inviting aroma of cooking.

'Your name, madam?' The voice was polite. Turning, Joanna was confronted by a man in full evening dress: a coat and tails, a silk shirt, a bow tie and brightly polished shoes. 'Your name, madam?' he repeated.

'Joanna Bradley,' she replied, much too surprised by his sudden appearance to say any more.

'Yes, you're expected,' he said. 'Your name's on the guest list and I'm to be your butler, madam. You're right on time. Well done! Come this way, please.'

'Wait!' said Joanna. 'You said I'm expected?'

'Yes, madam. Now please come quickly. Your table's reserved and drinks are about to be served. Come this way, please.'

'No, I won't,' she said stubbornly. 'You've made a mistake. I am Joanna Bradley, but I've never made a reservation on this airship. You've confused me with someone else. Forgive me for any inconvenience, but I must return home. My parents will be worried about me.'

'You are the Joanna Bradley who lives in Brixton, the daughter of Philip and Celia Bradley?' enquired the man, impatience creeping into his voice.

'Yes, I am, but I know nothing about this airship, nothing at all. I climbed the ladder because the airship appeared to be empty and I thought there was something wrong. My arrival here is a coincidence.'

'Coincidence, my dear, does not exist in the Captain's universe. Your arrival on this ship is the result of much careful planning. The Captain will explain. Please forgive us for any inconvenience, but the Captain will talk to you as soon as he's available and answer your questions. Meanwhile, I would be most grateful if you'd follow me to the banqueting

17

suite and ballroom. Your table's booked and drinks won't be served until your arrival. The other guests will be getting impatient.' He looked at his wristwatch. 'Oh dear!' he said. 'We're three minutes late already. It won't do, you know. Please, no more questions, there's a good girl. Just follow me.'

Joanna smarted at being referred to as a 'good girl'. She was sixteen and resented adults talking to her as if she were a child. 'Who does he think he is,' she thought, 'to give me orders?' If there had been an alternative, she would have disobeyed him, walked off in the opposite direction, but she had little choice. She trailed at his heels, resenting each elegant step that he made, longing for the day when she would be considered an adult.

The passage opened into a magnificent banqueting suite and ballroom. Chandeliers hung from the ceiling like constellations of glittering stars; the walls were wainscotted with elaborately carved panels; the wallpaper was a tasteful green embossed with a flower motif; the floor was made of wood, polished to such a lustre that the dancers were reflected in it.

It was not the grandeur of the surroundings that attracted Joanna, however, but the guests. Gathered about a raised dais on which the band played, and seated at tables on either side of the ballroom floor, was a most unusual assortment of guests. They were, or so it appeared to Joanna, all in fancy dress, wearing costumes from every corner of time. A tall Viking warrior stood next to a Samurai swordsman; a lady in a tight-fitting bodice and a huge rustling skirt danced with an admiral in full parade costume; a street boy from Calcutta, dressed only in dirty shorts, held the hand of an African girl in a garment of beads; and towering above them all was the tallest woman Joanna had ever seen. Her features were perfect: her eyes were large and as mysterious as distant worlds, her hair was black and short-cropped, and her skin was a delicate shade of violet. The fabric of her clothes had the texture of silk, tracing every curve and movement of her body like a synthetic skin. The colours of the fabric were as variable and exotic as an African sunset, changing with every shade of light and mood.

Joanna stood and gaped, her resentment against the butler forgotten. The woman's clothes made her appear as transparent as air, modestly covering her body, yet sensitively revealing her inner self. Suddenly aware of Joanna's gaze upon her, the woman turned and smiled, a bright, warm smile that promised friendship.

'Hurry up, please,' said Joanna's guide impatiently. 'Follow me to that table. That one there!' he said, pointing to a table already occupied by two guests. As Joanna approached, they looked up and studied her intently. Like the other guests at the ballroom, they were also in fancy dress. 'Your coat please, madam.' Joanna gave him her coat and sat down uncertainly between the two guests.

'Hello!' she said, but they were studying her too intently to reply. She was annoyed by their rudeness, but intrigued by their appearance and conversation.

'What century? Don't say anything. We'll guess,' said the older of the two.

'Say something. Just a few words will do. That'll give us a clue,' said the younger guest.

'Don't be stupid. You know as well as I do,' responded Joanna crossly. 'And why are you putting on those weird accents? Talk normally.'

The two strangers laughed. 'I bet you a new psycho-blaster with feelie probes that she's late twentieth century,' said the younger of the two. 'A real vintage era!' He leaned under the table and reappeared immediately: 'Yeah! She's late twentieth century all right. She's wearing denim jeans and trainers with a fluorescent strip. Hey, they aren't going to believe this back home: we've shared a table with a "prehistoric".'

'No more bets. I've lost three tonight already. You're the history buff, mega-brain, not me. And anyway, I don't think the girl understands. She's a newcomer.' He turned to Joanna and smiled engagingly. 'We're not joking,' he said. 'We actually come from 2492. My name is Edwin, and this is Thor. We're brothers. What's your name?'

'Joanna,' she said, studying their faces to see if she could detect any hint of deceit or playfulness, but there was none.

Their clothing was remarkable. Each brother wore a tightly fitted suit with enormous shoulder pads. The skin of their suits was criss-crossed by arteries of speeding light, and each brother wore a slender bracelet on his right wrist. Thor was skinny and intense; energy crackled from him like electricity. His nose was too small, his mouth too big, and his eyes too close together, but there was something attractive, even debonair, about his ugliness. Edwin, on the other hand, had the chiselled, manly features of a comic book hero, but his voice mocked the image. It was not a deep, booming earthquake of a voice, but a high falsetto, squeaking in his throat like a frightened mouse. The brothers, so different in appearance, had one physical trait in common: they had purple eyes!

'They must be wearing purple contact lenses. They're rich kids who can spend a fortune on fancy dress,' Joanna concluded, and felt a twinge of jealousy.

'All these people, including ourselves,' said Thor, with a sweep of his arm that embraced the ballroom 'are not in fancy dress. We're real.' There was a musical lilt to his voice that she found appealing.

'Not in fancy dress!' echoed Joanna in amazement. 'Where are they from? Who's responsible for bringing us all here?'

'The Captain,' said Edwin emphatically.

'Who?' asked Joanna.

'The Captain. The Captain of this airship. He's been doing this since the beginning of the world. All newcomers find it difficult to believe at first, but they all come round in the end. We did.'

'How?' demanded Joanna.

'We were cruising above Fifth Avenue at the height of about a thousand metres, coming home from the starball tournament, when . . .'

Thor interrupted his brother. 'She doesn't know what you're talking about. She's ancient history, Edwin. They couldn't cruise in the twentieth century. They had to rely on the petrol engine. You know, the thing that messed up the ozone layer and caused the poison rain in the twenty-first. Had to be banned. Remember?' Thor turned to Joanna. 'Sorry!' We're not used to talking to kids from the past. We take too much for granted. Our style of transport is very different from yours. These suits, for example, regulate our body temperature and enable us to cruise.'

'Cruise?' enquired Joanna.

'Fly,' replied Thor. 'The large shoulder pads are stabilisers. We just give the audio-beacon our proposed destination, intended speed and altitude, and away we go, riding the thermals like birds. The sensation is fantastic, especially in a full-blown gale.'

'The audio-beacon? What's that?' asked Joanna.

Thor pointed to his bracelet. 'This!' he said. 'You just speak into it like so.' He raised the bracelet to his lips and said, 'Lift mode two metres,' and shot up into the air. Everybody in the ballroom stopped what they were doing and stared.

'Get down!' said Edwin in an angry whisper. 'You're showing off again.' He looked apologetically at Joanna: 'Sorry about my brother. He's always playing the fool. Loves attracting attention.'

Joanna laughed. 'No need to apologise,' she replied, and then said very loudly, 'Fall mode two metres!' Down came Thor in an untidy heap, an expression of utter disbelief on his face.

'This is only supposed to respond to *my* voice,' he said. 'I'll have to take it back to the supplier.'

'Drinks?' said the clipped voice of a waiter.

'Yes please,' said Joanna, and she leaned to one side so that the waiter could place them on the table. Her drink was a refreshing punch flavoured with cinnamon and lemon. 'Delicious!' she sighed appreciatively, and then returned to the matter in hand. 'How did you get here?'

Edwin began again: 'We were cruising home from a starball tournament when . . .'

'Do you know what a starball tournament is?' asked Thor, silencing his brother.

'Tell me later,' she said. 'Now please continue the story.' She was aware that the brothers were competing for her attention; that they found her attractive. The idea pleased her, but at that moment their story was more important to her than flirtation.

'As we cruised above Fifth Avenue,' continued Edwin, 'a huge airship came from nowhere. One moment the sky was blank, and in the next, it suddenly appeared. At first we thought it was a new space cruiser on a test flight—they appear out of nowhere as well—but its appearance was too outlandish. Thor said it looked exactly like an early twentieth-century Zeppelin. Its windows were ablaze with light. "It must be a party," I said. They have a lot of weird parties in New York where we come from, so we decided to gatecrash and that's exactly how we arrived in this airship. At first, like you, we thought it was a fancy dress party, but then the . . .' The brothers suddenly fell silent, gazing at an approaching figure.

'It's the Captain,' whispered Thor reverently, his face glowing with joy. 'It's him!'

Joanna followed their gaze and saw a very ordinary person walking towards them. He didn't look particularly heroic or regal—hardly a popular superhero—but he radiated a life and wisdom older than the stars. His presence quietened the ballroom. A hush fell on the exotic gathering and every eye turned towards him. The silence was rich and deep, tingling with expectation. The people held their breath and waited.

The Captain approached Joanna. His skin was black with a scattering of lines about the eyes and corners of the mouth, his hair was greying, his features were large and irregular, but it was his eyes that captivated Joanna: dark, compassionate, burning with a wild and holy fire. They pierced Joanna, shattering her vanity, searching and testing her soul. The examination was over in a moment. The terrible, penetrating light vanished from his eyes, to be replaced by such warmth and boundless joy that Joanna felt as if she could look into them for ever.

'Thank you for coming, Joanna,' he said, holding out his hands in welcome. He said 'Thank you' as if he truly meant it; as if Joanna had done him a great honour. His voice was thrilling, a rich bass that shook with power and emotion.

Joanna was mesmerised. She had intended to tell the Captain off and ask him to take her home immediately; instead she took his outstretched hands in her own and held them. His palms were warm and she could feel the ticking of his pulse and the gentle pressure of his fingers.

'I'm sorry that you weren't notified about your reservation,' he said. 'You can go home now if you really want to. I can arrange transport immediately, but it will be a great pity. You see, I went to a lot of trouble to find you and draw you here.' His voice had such a penetrating yet attractive quality that Joanna found it difficult to resist. Steeling herself against its appeal, she reproached him.

'Why didn't you invite me to fly in your airship rather than parking outside my house and letting my curiosity do the rest?' The wisdom in the Captain's eyes startled her, but she didn't wait for an answer. Joanna knew that if she continued to stare into them, her resolve would vanish. She remembered the rope ladder writhing and lashing about like a snake in its death throes, the face of Dimrat, the awful groping hand, and her own terror. 'I was nearly killed on the ladder,' she said, fighting against the pleading in his eyes. 'What sort of captain are you? Are you like Dimrat? Do you enjoy playing games with people and seeing them suffer?'

An angry murmur of protest broke from the onlookers and rumbled threateningly towards her. 'Are you mad?' whispered Thor. 'He's the Captain!' But it was too late. Joanna had committed herself and could not turn back. 'I would describe what you've done as irresponsible; very irresponsible.'

The Captain ignored her questions. Instead, he stood up abruptly and addressed the crowd. 'This matter is none of your business,' he said sternly. 'Go back to your dancing and refreshments. This is a private matter.' He sat down again and turned the full power of his gaze upon her. 'Joanna,' he said, his voice cutting like a scalpel, 'you chose to climb the ladder and risk the journey to the airship. It was your choice, your responsibility, but even so, you were never, never alone. I am your guardian.' For a second, his face became transparent, a film of rippling light through which Joanna saw a multitude of forms: all of creation condensed into a moment. 'I was the mighty eagle that rescued you from Dimrat's torment.'

'But why do you want me? Why am I so important to you?'

'I have a task for you to accomplish, a very important task.' Joanna studied his eyes very carefully but there was no trace of mockery in them. 'I

24

want you to save a land, rescue it from a plague of darkness.'

Joanna was ambitious and determined, but she had never typecast herself as the saviour of a world. The obvious occurred to her: 'This is a game show, isn't it? My dad put you up to this. It's just the kind of thing he'd do. I'll kill him when I get home.' She looked about her for a concealed camera and film crew. 'It's a joke, isn't it?' she said, laughing with relief. Everything made sense: the airship, the weird costumes, the Captain and even the hologram of Dimrat. 'I even thought these two guys came from earth's future,' she said, looking at Thor and Edwin with an expression of fake anger on her face.

But nobody was smiling. Nobody! Her laughter faltered and then was gutted out like a tiny flame.

'This is not a joke, Joanna,' said the Captain gently. 'This is real.'

Joanna began to cry, hating herself for it. She was too ashamed to meet the eyes of the Captain, too afraid to show her vulnerability. For the first time in her life she felt really alone. 'If only Dad were here,' she thought, 'he'd know what to do.' Growing up had been very easy at home. Her parents were wise enough to allow her some independence, but were always there to help her when growing up became too difficult. She'd kicked against their discipline, argued for her own way, showed off if she didn't get it, and struggled to be someone other than Mr and Mrs Bradley's daughter, but the truth was she needed them. 'Growing up is tough,' she thought, 'but I can't run away, not for ever.'

She looked up and met the Captain's eyes. 'I'll go,' she said. 'Tell me what you want me to do.' And with these words, the child began to fade and the woman showed through.

5

The Hour of the Wolf

The airship voyaged across the sky, the vibration from its engine transferring along its length in minute tremors. Newly risen, the sun sailed on a parallel course, a ship of fire on a sea of blue. In one of the many cabins in the airship, Joanna slept, her diary open on her bedside table.

A dream came to her. She stood before a gallery of mirrors in an empty fairground. The woman at the turnstile was considerate and disarming: 'You go inside, dear. There's nothing to pay. It's all been sorted out. This way, please!' Once inside the gallery, an instinct made the girl turn. The woman's face was melting, the features running into each other, bubbling and hissing like rubber in a fire. From the ruined head burst the face of a wolf: jaws wide and slobbering, the eyes yellow and venomous with hate. They were Dimrat's eyes. The wolf howled and leaped towards her. The girl ran, the mirrors closing in about her like a forest of illusions. Each mirror had its own special trick. As she fled, the mirrors hurled their reflections at her: she was a headless corpse with a bloated body; a dwarf with a giant head; a cripple with deformed limbs. She moved so quickly that the reflections kaleidoscoped, each successive image swallowed by the next, until she was lost to herself.

At last the labyrinth opened into a central gallery. Dimrat was there, waiting, his image dancing in the encircling mirrors, driving out all other reflections. The girl turned to run, but there was nowhere to go. The exits had vanished. Dimrat sauntered towards her, his image leering at her from a hundred different mirrors. As he approached, the mirrors grew suddenly dark and Dimrat's reflection began to waver and fade. He stopped and looked about him, his eyes darting from one mirror to another, an expression of utter loathing on his face. 'Curse you!' he cried and bent the whole force of his will upon them, but to no avail. His image was driven from each, and in its place appeared the reflection of the Captain, his eyes burning with such a terrible and holy fire that the gallery blazed with light. The mirrors flamed like tiny novas and shattered, the fragments of glass exploding outwards like sparks. The gallery collapsed, falling around her in slow motion.

A voice reached down into the girl's nightmare. 'Madam! Madam! Is there something wrong? Do you need assistance?' The voice was a long way off, but she held it desperately, clung to it like a piece of flotsam in the shipwreck of her world. She raced back through the shattering mirrors, clambered over the turnstile and ran towards it.

'Madam, are you sure there's nothing wrong? Are you all right?'

Joanna opened her eyes and looked into the face of the butler. 'Yes, I think so,' she said. 'I must have been dreaming.'

'It must have been a very strange dream, Madam, if you don't mind my saying so. You were kicking, fighting and crying out like a mad thing. Are you sure you're all right?' His concern was so obviously genuine that Joanna felt guilty.

'He's not half as stuck-up as he seems,' she thought, 'and I was so nasty to him yesterday.'

Sunlight flooded her room, a wide river of golden light that drowned the last shadows and lingering dreams of night. 'Madam, I have been instructed to give you breakfast in bed,' said the butler, and he offered Joanna a silver tray. The delicious aroma of

27

fried bacon, sausages, eggs and mushrooms filled the cabin, awakening her appetite instantly.

'Mmm! Thanks! This is my favourite,' she said, as she squirted tomato ketchup over her eggs and sausages.

'Madam,' said the butler apologetically, 'we'll be arriving at your destination in twenty minutes. The Captain won't be able to see you off—some urgent business has come up—but he's given you this backpack with a few useful things in it. He said that you'll need them. Now I'll leave you to eat and dress in peace. You'll find the bathroom through the door to the right of your bed. May I recommend that you shower. You don't have time to use the bath. Thank you, Madam. If you need anything, just ring.' The butler pointed to a braided bell cord hanging above the bed. 'That's it, Madam. One pull will be sufficient, and thank you, thank you once again.'

Joanna opened the door of the bathroom and looked within appreciatively. 'Not bad for a city girl!' she thought, as she admired the luxurious interior. The floor was of white marble, the rear and side walls were decorated with pale blue tiles, and the far wall was a window looking out on a vista of sun, blue sky and foaming bubble-bath clouds. In the centre of the room, indented in the floor like a rock pool, was a huge crystal bath, and above it, the shower jets hung down in clusters like palm leaves. 'The butler's okay,' she thought, noticing a sponge bag on the chair. 'He even left toothpaste and a brush. Fancy having my own butler!' She laughed and mimicked his voice: 'Thank you, Madam. Thank you!' Her friends would love it when she imitated him. She grew suddenly thoughtful: 'But who'll believe me? They'll think I'm mad if I tell them about the Captain and the airship, and who'll ever believe that I met two guys from the future?'

After showering, Joanna snuggled into a bathrobe,

28

sighing with pleasure as the soft, warm fleece caressed her skin. Returning to her cabin, she undid the backpack and placed the contents neatly on her bed: lightweight cooking equipment, freeze-dried meals, waterproof matches, a Swiss Army penknife, a sleeping bag, a mattress, a dome tent, walking shoes, toiletries, a rain suit and two changes of clothes. Joanna marvelled at the Captain's choice. 'These clothes are really me,' she thought and tried them on. She 'cat-walked' to the mirror, her movements lithe and rhythmic, and gazed at her reflection critically. The fit and colour of each garment matched her perfectly. 'I couldn't have chosen better myself,' she thought, and was grateful for the Captain's thoughtfulness. Rummaging in the backpack to see if she had missed anything, Joanna found four bars of her favourite chocolate and a wide-toothed comb in a side pocket.

Her impromptu fashion show was interrupted by a polite knock on the door. 'Are you ready, Madam? It's time to go. Quickly, please.' There was something strange about the butler's voice, but Joanna was too distracted to notice. 'Coming!' she called, and struggled into the straps of the backpack. The butler was waiting for her, his face lowered respectfully, his features hidden. 'After you, along the corridor, Madam. Take the first on the left. The landing exit is at the end of the corridor. You'll see.'

There was no turning back now. She had agreed to carry out the Captain's mission. The exit loomed ahead of her, a brilliant rectangle of light in the shell of the ship. Behind her, barring her escape, was the butler, his deft, unobtrusive footsteps echoing softly in the corridor.

The last seven hours had the quality of a dream. A series of incredible events had lifted her out of her very ordinary life in South London, and thrust her into a dangerous adventure. As she walked along the

29

corridor, her mind replayed each sequence of the story.

'I wish the Captain had come and said goodbye to me,' she thought sadly. After her conversation with him, she had danced with Edwin and Thor, enjoying the effect that she had on both of them. She smiled at the memory, a roguish light dancing briefly in her eyes. And what of the giant woman, Valsa, with her wise, ancient eyes and poetic speech: 'I am a Watcher, the last of earth's human remnant.' Her voice was deep and restful. 'In my time, the sun has grown old and the world with it. Soon, very soon, the Captain will return and set our galaxy ablaze, and from its ruin will arise a new and fairer world, a brighter sun. You come from a younger world, Joanna. Countless aeons separate us, but here on the Captain's ship we can be friends.'

When Joanna had become too exhausted to dance or talk any longer, the butler had escorted her to her cabin, given her a towel and a nightdress, and retired with a discreet and kindly: 'Sleep well, Madam.'

Joanna reached the exit and looked out. The blue sky stretched endlessly before her, a blue so pure that she thought she had come to the edge of the world and was looking off. Beneath her, in grim contrast, was a boiling cauldron of grey cloud, overflowing the land below, hiding it from view.

'Goodbye, Joanna!'

Joanna shuddered and swung round, recognising immediately the cruel mockery of the voice, but strong hands picked her up and forced her to the door. The exit opened and the wind tore into her, seizing her with a hideous force, catapulting her from the airship and tossing her into its slipstream like a tiny feather. As she hurtled downwards—the seething, demonic cloud racing to meet her—the voice screeched in her ears again: 'Welcome to the grey land!'

It was the voice of Dimrat!

6

The Fugitive

Sky and land were bleached of colour. Above him the clouds gathered, not soft white clouds bobbing in a sea of blue, but angry, volcanic clouds, belching from the horizon and streaming towards him like a lava flow. Distant but drawing ever nearer, he could hear the sound of the chase: the screams and howls of the nazdargs and the faint shouts of men. The giant was hidden from his pursuers by a jagged promontory of rock that straddled the plain like a stegosaurus from earth's prehistory.

The giant raised his binoculars and studied his pursuers. He pitied the nazdargs. Like the giants, they had been created in the laboratories of Dimrat, but unlike his race, they had never rebelled against their master. More beast than man, the nazdargs had been formed in artificial wombs and then unleashed upon the world. The giant smiled, a sad, crooked smile, part self-mockery and part humour. 'Dimrat made us,' he reflected, 'but he never owned our souls, never defeated us. Even when the last of us is slain, we'll still remind him of his impotence. He'll remember us and hear the Captain laughing at him.'

For weeks the giant had been a fugitive, hunted by Dimrat and the president's secret police. An instinct had drawn him back to the mountains, the last refuge of his people. Here his family had died, the memories sealed in his mind like bodies in a crypt.

The nazdargs drew closer, plumes of dust erupting from their speeding feet. The giant lowered his binoculars and crouched down. A solitary wild flower caught his attention, its petals bright with colour and its leaves a rich green tinged with purple at their edges.

31

Forgetting the racing nazdargs and his own danger, the giant uttered a cry of wonder and flung himself upon the ground, his face so close to the tiny flower that it shivered in his breath. The giant reached out and stroked the petals with his fingertips. 'A miracle,' he whispered, his voice awed and gentle. 'Colour has returned to the land.' He had been told that the world had once been full of colours, but he often doubted. Now he knew for certain that the story was true. His stone grey face glistened with joy as he examined the flower, fingering it reverently like a priceless gem, observing the subtlety of its colours. His mother had taught him their names—red, blue, orange, gold, silver, magenta, saffron, purple, green, brown—forbidden names, but he lacked the knowledge to match name with colour.

'My mother would have welcomed this day,' he reflected sadly. He still dreamed of her at night: a tall, graceful woman walking across a wide meadow dipped in light and sown with dancing grass, the sunlight burning on her face. In the dream he called to her, but she never answered him. Once he cried so loudly that she faltered and searched the meadow with her eyes, but the bright sun hid him from her.

The most enduring memory of his mother was her voice, enchanting him with stories of the land before Dimrat stole its colour: 'The sky was not always grey, my son, but a vast canvas splashed with colour—one day, black storm clouds thundering across it, maddened by the whiplash of forked lightning, and on another, a deep blue flecked with white foam. Yes, and flowers flocked our gardens like birds with painted wings and the trees and fields were a thousand shades of green. If only you could have seen it, my son!'

Closing his eyes, the giant took the colours from the flower, and in his mind painted the world. 'Oh, what a beautiful place it must have been,' he thought, and he felt a song stirring in his heart.

Flying in tight formation like a locust swarm, the helicopter gunships raced around the shoulder of the mountain, their whirling blades beating against the sky like thunder. The giant sprang to his feet and faced them, his body protected by Kevlar armour and his huge gun balanced and steady in his hands. Searchlights blazed—shafts of light streaked towards him, trapping him in a net of interlacing beams. An amplified voice boomed down: 'Surrender, Rumbold. Throw down your weapons or we'll kill you.'

The giant was tempted to shoot out the searchlights and scatter the gunships in a burst of fire. He had done it many times before: an image in his laser sight, a sudden pressure on the trigger, a fireball, and a gunship would plummet from the sky.

Dimrat had lectured the giants on their destiny: 'You are my dancers, my lovely dancers, and your dance is a ballet of death.' His voice was soft and cruel. 'You do not need to be taught its steps. I have recorded them in your genes and their rhythms beat in your blood. Have you ever wondered why you are huge, strong, fast and utterly fearless? It is because I forged you as my weapon. You kill because it is your nature to kill. Death is your trade.'

'Dimrat, you're mistaken again,' whispered the giant, and he threw down his gun and lifted his arms in surrender. He loathed killing, as had all his people, but he had been forced to it.

The down draught of the helicopter screws tore into him and beat against the tiny flower. 'Little flower, I thank you. You have given me hope and shown me the beauty of the world.' The land was grey about him, but Rumbold knew that it was merely sleeping. He looked at the tiny flower and marvelled at its toughness. Lifting his voice defiantly, the giant sang, the forbidden notes rising above the thunder of the gunships.

'Stop your singing. It is forbidden!' commanded the voice, but the giant continued. Reaching the foot of the escarpment, the nazdargs scaled it and leapt towards him, but his song dashed their advance, awakening the knowledge that they too were partly human. Silently they circled Rumbold, jerking their heads as if to shake the melody from them.

Rumbold was still singing when the plastic bullet slammed into his head.

*   *   *

'Rumbold, your behaviour has caused us grave concern.'

The giant lay on a rough stone floor, his face swollen and disfigured. He could hear the voice, but it was a long way off. He struggled towards it, but as he drew nearer, the agony in his head increased.

'Not only are you guilty of treason, but worse, you do what is forbidden: you sing!'

Rumbold opened his eyes. The room tilted and shook for a few moments and then a face came slowly into focus, a face as perfect and as deadly as a carnivorous orchid.

'Hello, Mr President!' croaked the giant ironically, and he struggled to sit upright. The room blurred and waves of agony crashed against the giant's skull. He groaned and touched his face, searching for damage with fingertips as sensitive as any surgeon's. 'There are no fractures, only serious bruising,' he thought, and smiled ruefully to himself: 'Thank you, Dimrat. A normal man would be dead.'

'Rumbold, you have given my government a lot of trouble.' The voice was chiding. 'You rebel against your master, Dimrat, and then complain when we punish you. If a dog is mad, what do we do?' He looked at Rumbold for a few seconds, his face suave and his eyes mild, even gentle: 'We put him out of his misery!' The weak, grey sunlight smoked through

34

the bars of the cell window. The president took a syringe from his pocket and held it up to the light, examining the level of the liquid within. He squirted a little from the needle point, the droplets trickling down his delicate fingers.

'But if the dog is tame,' countered the giant, 'and intruders attempt to rob and burn his real master's house, would he be wrong to turn upon them?'

'Intruders, Rumbold? Are you referring to Lord Dimrat and his government of which I am the elected president?'

'Elected president!' guffawed the giant, and then stopped suddenly, the pain in his head silencing his laughter. 'Elected by whom? By Dimrat? By the nazdargs? By your secret police who reward disagreement with torture or a bullet? By your puppet politicians who voice your policies like ventriloquists' dummies? Kill me, Mr President, but don't insult me with your empty propaganda.'

The president smiled, a soft indulgent smile, as if he were dealing with a difficult child. 'Propaganda, Rumbold, is merely a series of stories that are circulated to make people think that things are better than they are, a camouflage that hides the world. We are not interested in propaganda. We don't need it. We are the creators of truth. We have the power, yes the power, to reinvent the world. If you had been wise, Rumbold, you could have joined us.' He glanced at the syringe sadly.

'If this is wisdom, let me be a fool. You kill the world and replace it with a land as grey as mildew. And if that isn't enough, you forbid song and laughter and crush the human spirit. What sort of world have you reinvented, Mr President?'

'A world without war and hunger, Rumbold, a perfect machine of a world where each cog rotates without questioning its purpose. Colour and song are subversive. They encourage dreams. The world is only a windowless box surrounded by darkness. If we permit singing and colour, the people become discontented. Think, Rumbold! Your mother told you the forbidden stories of the past: the wars, the famines, the unrest, the revolutions, the religious fanatics, the exploitation and the misery. We offer a new world, a place where the excesses of the human spirit are curbed and redirected.' Rumbold recognised with a sudden, cold perception that the president was not mad but completely sane.

'I have seen the old world in a flower,' he whispered, as much to himself as to the president. It was the only argument he could find to deny the president's logic.

'The giant is poetic,' said the president mockingly, 'and very obscure.'

Rumbold ignored his sarcasm. 'I have seen the old world in a flower,' he repeated wistfully, his voice gentle and full of dreams. 'Yes, I have heard of the old world, but give me that world, Mr President, with all its weaknesses and folly, and you can keep this land of ghosts and broken dreams.'

'You shall have your wish,' said the president, and he advanced towards the giant, the syringe held steady like a scorpion's tail.

The giant didn't resist. He closed his eyes and remembered the flower. It shone in his mind like a dazzling star, but as he gazed upon it, its brightness was eclipsed by the face of a man. The man's brow was crowned with stars, and his eyes filled the universe with light. Rumbold began to sing, the notes spilling from his heart and converging in a flood of joy and freedom.

He heard the warning, 'It is forbidden to sing!' but it was faint and far away—and he felt the sting of the needle in his arm, but life and death were of no importance to him. He was still singing when darkness seized him and silenced his voice—not a cold, empty darkness, but a wide river filled with stars and angels.

The president looked at the unconscious giant and turned and left the cell, the notes of Rumbold's song following him along the passage, keeping time with the beat of his steps. He passed a group of nazdargs. 'Take him to the cage!' he commanded and passed on.

7

The Busker

Joanna fell shrieking through the air, the grey clouds rising to embrace her and the wind buffeting her body. She hit the clouds, vanished, and reappeared below them, a tiny figure with arms and legs splayed out, crucified against the sky. She heard herself screaming, but the sound seemed a long way off. Fear numbed her and drove her inwards to that silent country of the soul. She was two people: one hurtled downwards with a scream trailing her descent like a tail of fire, and the other was calm and detached, watching the earth pitch towards her in slow motion: outwardly a shrieking girl; inwardly, a spy lens observing herself and all reality with a terrible and brilliant clarity. 'I screamed,' she wrote later, 'but inwardly I tumbled through a dream.'

And then she was no longer falling, but floating above the grey land.

'You're safe! You're safe, Joanna! Don't be afraid!' She had retreated so deeply into herself that the words were a lifetime away. 'Joanna, it's Edwin. You're safe.'

And then another voice followed the first.

'Man, that was fancy flying. You hit her just at the optimum angle and used her momentum to break the fall. Text book stuff. Is she okay?'

'She's catatonic. The screaming's stopped, but her eyes are blank and she's not responding to my voice.'

'Let me try!'

'Keep your hands off, little brother. She's already had one terrible scare and another might kill her.'

'Hey, Edwin, I might not be as pretty as you, but let me remind you that I'm the one with the qualification in rare planetary diseases. The girl needs a professional. Hand her over. And anyway, if you continue to hug her like that, she'll suffocate.'

'Quit the banter, Thor, and let's surf the thermals. Vertigo will kill the girl if we don't touch down on terrafirma.'

'I'm okay,' said Joanna weakly. The good-natured repartee of the brothers had drawn her back to herself. 'Thanks! Thanks for saving me!' Then suddenly words tumbled from her lips: 'Dimrat threw me from the airship. I thought I was going to die. I shut my eyes and pretended that I was dreaming. When I was younger, I often dreamed that I was on a train that wouldn't stop. It went faster and faster until everything I looked at from the window sped by me in a blur of colour. I felt like that when I was falling. My life sped by me in a blur and I remembered things that I'd forgotten, silly things like tearing my new dress on the garden fence. I wondered if death would hurt, or would it be like the injection before I had my tonsils out: one moment awake, and then nothing, no pain or dreams, nothing at all. Then when I thought about "nothing" I wanted to live for ever. And suddenly I saw it: I was actually going to die. I was about to collide head-on with death and there was nothing I could do to avoid it. Death was really going to happen to me, and I would never see a whale, or become a marine biologist, or fall in love and marry, or see my dad and mum again. But then you rescued me. How did you know that Dimrat had thrown me from the airship?'

'It was the Captain,' said Edwin. 'He threw open the door of our cabin and shouted: "Save Joanna!" He pointed at the outer wall of our cabin and it opened like a hatch. The wind seized us and we were hurled into the slipstream of the airship. Fortunately, I saw you before you hit the cloud cover and I power-dived at a hundred and fifty mezalons to intercept your fall.'

'You're a slow learner, Edwin. She doesn't understand the meaning of "mezalons".' Thor made a quick calculation: 'He means that he was travelling at 753.02739 mph. He'll never tell you, but he risked his life to save you.'

'Thank you, Edwin,' she said gratefully.

'I'm beginning to regret it already,' he replied. 'Let go of my neck before you strangle me.' Joanna unloosed her fingers from his neck. 'You'll be quite safe if you don't struggle. Try to relax!'

Edwin spoke into his control bracelet and they slowly descended. Joanna felt a slight jolt as Edwin's feet touched the earth, and then he placed her gently on the ground. 'Goodbye, Joanna. We can't stay. The Captain instructed us to return immediately.' Thor joined him, and both young men looked at her regretfully. 'We hate to leave you like this, but the Captain knows what he's doing.' Thor and Edwin hugged her and then wrenched themselves away. Joanna watched them until they disappeared into the clouds.

The land about her was grey and colourless and the air was rotten with the stench of decay. A few stunted trees broke the monotony of the skyline, and in the distance she could see the ragged outline of a town, a dirty pall of pollution hanging above it like a mushroom cloud. Apart from a few gaunt cows who were too listless to be curious about her presence, the fields were empty and neglected.

Beyond the field, Joanna could see the dull ribbon of a road. 'If I don't take action soon,' she thought, 'I'll give up.'

Joanna trudged silently along the road, her spirit dulled by the terrible melancholy of the country. When the Captain had asked her to go and bring the colours back to this land, it had seemed possible, but now she was oppressed by the task. It was a new experience for Joanna. She had strolled through childhood and early adolescence with the easy grace and confidence of the successful, but now she felt weak and inadequate. There was no list of instructions to guide her, and no friends or family to advise her on the quest. Moreover, she knew that Dimrat was responsible for removing the colour from the land, and the thought of meeting him again terrified her. As she trudged along, she struggled to invent a plan of action: 'I'll go to the police and say that I've been sent by the Captain to restore colour to the land. But what would I say if they ask me how I intend to do it? Probably it's better to make discreet inquiries first: Could you tell me how this country turned grey? Is it possible to bring the colour back? How would one attempt to do this? Is there a political party or organisation who're tackling the problem? If so, how can I join it? And then when I've gathered sufficient information, I can volunteer to help.'

Joanna's plans were interrupted by the appearance of a house. The road swung sharply to the right, and as she rounded the bend, she saw a shambling two-storey apartment. Several of the windows were boarded up, but smoke trickled from the chimney and a television aerial hung rakishly from the roof. Joanna opened the gate and walked cautiously along the garden path. She rapped on the door with her knuckles and heard the owner shuffling within. A key ground in the lock and the door squealed open, but only wide enough for the owner to peer out.

Joanna caught sight of a pair of hostile eyes and a smudge of features before the door crashed shut in her face. 'Go away, ghost!' howled the woman. 'Colours do not exist. Do you hear me? Colours do not exist! Go away!' Too shocked and hurt to reply, Joanna looked dumbly at herself. The land and everything in it was painted a dusty grey, but she had retained her colour.

As she approached the town, houses became more numerous, but the response was always the same: doors slammed shut, children fled from her in terror, people cursed and told her to go away, and stones and other missiles pelted down on her. Just as she was about to turn back, a familiar voice said: 'Hello, Joanna, may I accompany you?' She swung round and there was the Captain. He had exchanged his dress uniform for a wide-brimmed sombrero and a colourful Mexican poncho, and a guitar case was slung across his back.

Joanna's depression left her immediately. 'You look like a tourist who's arrived at the wrong destination,' she said with a chuckle in her voice. 'You don't need that hat. There's no chance of sunburn here! Why have you come?'

'To keep an eye on you and teach these good people to appreciate music!'

'I hope they like music more than they like colours.'

'They haven't had much experience of either, so I'm here to begin their education.'

His presence filled Joanna with hope and confidence. Before his arrival she had felt her mission was hopeless and had been angry with him for sending her on it. Now he was here, her task was less daunting. The Captain radiated such power and joy that his presence seemed to toss aside the grey shroud that covered the land.

The rumour of the Captain and Joanna's arrival reached the town before them. Doors were bolted against them and the streets were empty, yet the vacant windows bristled with inquisitive eyes. The only sounds they heard were the faint scurrying of rats' feet and the rustle of litter blown about in sporadic flurries of wind. The town watched their progress in silence.

'They don't seem very friendly,' said Joanna in a sharp, sarcastic voice. 'They're obviously very suspicious of strangers, especially the coloured variety.'

'Don't be hard on them. They'll soon warm up once they hear a few songs and see my light show. I intend to plant a song today that will grow and fill this country.'

The street opened into a wide square surrounded by shabby yet magnificent municipal buildings.

'These places have seen better days,' remarked Joanna. 'The columns and statues are crumbling. Look! The old gas street lamps are still standing and there was once a fountain in that filthy pond. This place must have looked fantastic before it fell into decay.'

'It did, Joanna. I remember this square before the coming of Dimrat. It was the showpiece of the world. Believe me, the time is near when it will live again and be more beautiful than ever. Men and women will stand where we are standing now and will tell the story of the doom of Dimrat to their children.' The Captain spoke with such assurance that Joanna never doubted him. 'Come,' he commanded, 'and let's stand by that statue and give a concert that will be remembered for a thousand years.'

A chord in a minor key announced the beginning of the concert. The sound trembled in the air above them and then floated sadly across the square. The Captain paused, then his fingers suddenly danced across the strings and notes cascaded around them like stars. He spun the notes into a melody and sang of the beauty of the land before the coming of Dimrat.

He looked at Joanna, smiled and then raised his voice an octave. Lightning forked in the sky and everything it touched resumed its proper colour, but only for a moment: grey tiles on a nearby roof turned orange; a garden was painted with bright colours; a tree was struck and flamed with greens and browns; and a patch of sky turned blue, and the sun within it white gold too bright to look upon.

Faces appeared at windows, furtive faces that spied on them from gaps in curtains and half-open doors. A group of ragged children appeared at the edge of the square and looked awkwardly towards the Captain. He welcomed them with a smile and they lost their shyness and ran towards him, chattering like a flock of birds. The children were dirty and neglected, and some of them looked very ill. A tall boy with a deformed arm called out: 'We're not supposed to sing, mate. It's forbidden. If we sing they throw us in borstal or send us to the uranium mines to work. If we're sent there, we never come back. My sister had her tongue cut out for singing.' He pushed the mute girl towards the Captain. 'Open your mouth, Lisa, and let the bloke see.' But Lisa clamped her lips shut and looked fearfully into the Captain's face.

'You don't need to be afraid of me, Lisa.' His voice was soft and magical. 'They've taken your tongue, but the music is still inside you. They can't take that away.' Very gently, he laid his hand on her cheek and looked deep into her eyes. 'Don't be afraid, little one,' he whispered, 'you can sing with me now.' The Captain's eyes were full of love.

'Hey, mate, how do you do that trick with lightning?' asked a short girl in a dress much too large for her. She wiped her nose with the back of her hand and continued her inquiry: 'And what do you call the thing that happens when the lightning hits something and changes it into something nicer?'

'Shut up, Beatrice, you little trouble maker,' shouted

43

a boy with a crew cut. 'If you open your big mouth and let this story out, they'll take out our eyes at the state hospital. Do you remember what happened to Robin? He told his teacher that he'd seen something that wasn't grey, and the next thing we knew, he'd been taken away by the nazdargs.' The children shivered, and their eyes grew large with fear.

'Children! Children!' reproached the Captain. 'This is a concert and not a school lesson. Listen to me very carefully.' He leaned forward and beckoned the children to come closer with a movement of his index finger. The sombrero and the Mexican poncho gave him a comical quality. The children lost their fear and crowded round him, their faces upturned expectantly. 'If you listen to the music with both ears wide open,' he whispered, 'all your questions will be answered and the adults won't be able to hurt you.'

'Concerts are illegal,' said the boy with the crew cut in an accusing voice.

'That's an evil law and evil laws should be resisted,' replied the Captain. 'I promise you that music will fill this land from end to end and you'll all live to hear it. Okay, no more questions. Let's play and fill the town with music.' And with that remark, his fingers danced on the guitar strings again and his voice rolled through the town and on and on across the land.

Joanna was enthralled. She sat on hard paving stones with her chin resting on her knees and gazed at the Captain with eyes full of dreams and hope. His songs entered into her, the beauty of each melody writing the lyric on her heart and memory. Her voice accompanied his until she realised that thousands more were singing with them. Streams of people flowed into the square and filled it. The power of the Captain's songs and the anonymity and courage that a large crowd gives to people unloosed their tongues. As they sang, the lightning wreaked havoc on the grey and lashed the land with colour. But it wasn't the singing crowd or the wild lightning that Joanna remembered most of all, but little Lisa. With one hand resting on the Captain's leg, she stood and sang, her face aglow with joy.

The sound was distant, a faint throbbing, but it grew quickly in volume to a dull thunder. Hysterical screams and shouts of fear shook the crowd. The people scattered from the square in panic, bursting into the exit roads and pedestrian walkways in crushed clusters of bodies.

The gunships flew low over the rooftops, their searchlights driving into the crowd in solid wedges of light. Sirens wailed, machine guns stuttered into life and tear gas canisters were tossed into the crowd, exploding in spurts of venomous smoke. 'This concert is illegal. Disperse quietly or severe action will be taken,' intoned an amplified voice from the leading gunship.

Joanna stood alone beneath the shadow of the statue, too shocked to think about escape. The crowd had fled the square, the bodies of their injured comrades abandoned on the cobbles like stranded fish. She searched for the Captain, but the only sign that she could find of him was his crushed sombrero. 'Why do you always leave me when I need you most?' she thought.

A gunship dipped towards her and its searchlight trapped her in a circle of light. 'Don't move!' commanded an amplified voice. 'Stay exactly where you are.' Even in the grey gloom of day, the beam was still blinding. Joanna heard the tramp of feet, the circle of light was breached in many places, and savage, half-human creatures rushed in upon her.

The nazdargs carried Joanna to the waiting gunship.

8

The Crime of Colour

Joanna shivered as the castle drew closer. From a distance, it looked like a giant hand, its cluster of towers poking into the sky like fingers. She could see it clearly through the nose of the gunship, swelling with the speed of their approach until it filled the horizon. She could smell the rank stench of the nazdargs in the compartment behind her and hear the croak of their voices. The pilot sat emotionless in the next seat, his eyes as cold as shards of ice. Aware that she was looking at him, he raised his voice above the scream of the blades: 'Welcome to your new home. Study it well. You will never see it again from the outside.'

The gunship swept over the battlements of the castle and came to rest in the courtyard below. Joanna snatched up her backpack and thrust her arms through the shoulder straps.

'Get up and follow us. The president is waiting for you in the Hall of the People,' commanded the nazdarg sergeant, a huge, crippled creature with a curved spine and the long, sinewy arms of an ape. He spoke as if each word had shattered in his throat and he was spitting out the splinters. 'Come!' he commanded and reached for her.

Joanna dodged the pawing hand and jumped from the gunship. She allowed the nazdargs to escort her into the bleak interior of the castle. They marched her along a short cul-de-sac of a passage which ended abruptly in a set of double doors. The sergeant knocked once and then shouted: 'We bring the prisoner.' The doors swung open and Joanna was thrust into a large hall. It was comfortably furnished, and a huge fire burned in the grate. The nazdargs retreated, closing the doors behind them.

'So, the freak has arrived. We've been expecting you.' The speaker looked at her with tiny, greedy eyes, and the folds of fat that hung beneath his chin wobbled as he spoke. Joanna was repulsed. He reminded her of a goblin who had been blown up to three times his normal size.

'I'm not a freak. I'm a normal person. The Captain sent me to help you bring back colour to the land.'

'Colour!' cried the fat man, his high, feminine voice squeaking in outrage. 'She has the audacity to speak of colour in this hall of government.' He turned to the assembled company: 'Mr President, ladies and gentlemen, what other evidence do we need? She's confessed her guilt and spoken the awful word of blasphemy.' His lips puckered and he spat the word out in a whisper: 'Colour!' The folds of fat on his body shook with distaste. He lifted a hand and slapped Joanna across the face. Smack! The blow was weak but the rings on his stubby fingers stung her and left tiny marks on her cheek. The pain and humiliation of it detonated Joanna's temper.

'Keep your hands off me or you'll regret it!'

'You threaten me?' he said disbelievingly, and his eyes vanished into the pouches of fat that rimmed them as if sucked down by quicksand. He turned to the crowd: 'She's a devil! A witch! Did you hear her? She threatened me!' His tiny eyes reappeared and they were blurred with tears. 'She must be punished,' he said brokenly, but before he could slap her again, Joanna slipped a leg behind his ankles and hurled her weight at his chest. The fat man tumbled on his back and lay there like an upended turtle. A snigger of disrespectful laughter swept across the gathering.

A hand fell on Joanna's shoulder. 'I'm sorry about the behaviour of my deputy president. I've been wanting to meet you.' Joanna swung round and

47

looked into the grey eyes and slender features of the president. 'What is your name?' he inquired kindly.

Joanna was about to reply when the fat man interrupted her: 'Kill the brat! Chop her up as nazdarg food! How dare she attack the deputy president of our great and glorious land. Did you see what she did to me?'

'I did,' said the president, 'and in future, treat our guests with more courtesy.'

The fat man looked up at the president in astonishment and his small lips trembled.

'Get off the floor, man, and preserve some dignity,' ordered the president sternly, 'and save your tears for the day when I sack you from office.' The president watched his deputy waddle to his seat and then turned to Joanna: 'If his manners don't improve, he'll be serving a life sentence in a health farm. Now, my dear, tell me your name and why you're here.'

'My name's Joanna and I was sent here by the Captain to bring colour back to the land.'

The president grimaced at the mention of 'colour'. 'Please don't mention that word here. It's forbidden. Who is this person called the Captain?'

'I don't know very much about him. He travels the world in an airship and has the ability to bring people together from every part of time. He's a remarkable person.'

'I'm not sure I agree with you,' said the president in a voice as soft as silk. 'He seems to be a meddler, a "do-gooder" who'd be better off looking after his own affairs. Did he have anything to do with the open-air concert?'

'Yes, he was the singer.'

'I thought as much. A number of people were injured and trampled to death after that concert. Your Captain appears to be very irresponsible.'

'It was the arrival of your gunships—not the Captain's concert—that caused the panic.'

The president ignored her: 'Yes, this Captain fellow is a menace. We'd like you to appear on TV and denounce him publicly as a dangerous criminal. Moreover, we'd like you to tell our viewers that he enticed you to wear objects that were not in conformity with the law.'

'What do you mean?'

'We'd like you to confess that he made you, forced you, to relinquish the grey and adorn your face and body with wicked deceptions. If you oblige, you'll be the honoured guest of my government.' He made the request as if he was granting a favour. His manner was charming and he was so persuasive that Joanna found him difficult to resist.

'And if I don't?'

'That alternative is unthinkable. You *will*!'

Joanna studied the president. He was very tall and handsome, and he used both qualities to his advantage. He looked down at Joanna, making her feel small and inferior. His eyes were mild, not mad and fiery like those of a fanatic, and he spoke fluently as if each word was dipped in oil, yet Joanna felt that he was evil. She groped for words and ideas to clothe her misgivings: 'He's like a tree: outwardly strong and beautiful, but the trunk is rotten and hollow.'

'You cannot change what I am,' she spoke out. 'You cannot make me grey and drab like the rest of you. The lie will be obvious to anybody who sees me.'

'Nobody will ever see you, my dear. You'll remain in this wonderful castle for the rest of your life as our guest. We have a number of excellent guest rooms in the lower levels of the castle. I think you call them dungeons in your country. If you co-operate, our Lord Dimrat may even change your complexion. He has a wonderful way with people!'

'Why are you so afraid of colour?'

'Please don't repeat that terrible word.'

'But why? What is so evil about colour? The world that I come from is bright with colour.'

'The belief in colour,' said the president, his nose twitching as if he had smelled an unpleasant odour, 'is evidence of insanity. It is a dangerous idea that can unsettle the ignorant and foolish.'

'Look at me!' pleaded Joanna. 'My hair is black, my eyes brown, my skin is olive, and look at my clothes. They're all different colours. How do you explain me?'

The president smiled and his eyes were mild: 'You do not exist!'

Joanna was stunned: 'But I do exist. We're talking, and you can reach out a hand and touch me. Are you colour blind?'

Ignoring her question, the president continued: 'We have decreed that colour does not exist. The logic is simple. If colour does not exist, then you do not exist. Let's return to my proposal. Will you appear on TV and denounce the Captain?'

Joanna couldn't believe what she was hearing. 'But if you think that I don't exist, why invite me to appear on TV and tell your viewers that the Captain is a dangerous fraud?'

'Young lady, your questions are becoming irritating. If I say you don't exist, you mustn't argue with me, but accept my word on it. As the president of this country, I have the power to say what exists and what doesn't exist. You don't exist, but a number of simple-minded people believe that you do. How do we resolve this little problem? We allow the people to see your imaginary image on TV and hear you saying that this thing called "colour" does not exist.'

'But I do exist, and colour exists,' protested Joanna, 'and I refuse to denounce the Captain on TV.'

Silence fell on the hall, a silence full of menace and foreboding. The president sighed: 'Have it your own way, Joanna. As a non-person, you have no rights under the law. We can do with you as we like. Resistance is useless. You will denounce the Captain. Dimrat will see to that!' He walked to the double doors and gently pushed them open. 'Nazdargs,' he called, 'take the girl to the cage.'

The nazdargs marched her back along the passage and into the courtyard. 'That will be your home until Dimrat returns,' croaked the sergeant, and he pointed upwards. Joanna saw the cage. It was suspended from the highest of the castle's towers, and the wind shook it and shrieked through its bars as if the cage itself was screaming.

The cage was lowered on a system of pulleys. Joanna was seized from behind by the nazdargs and thrown into it. An enormous man crouched in the corner of the cage, his arms and legs manacled to the floor. Joanna stifled a scream and slunk into the opposite corner. The giant was asleep, his head pillowed in his arms, and his breathing was strong and regular. His head and face were hairless and as smooth as polished marble, and he had a hooked nose.

The giant awoke and gazed at Joanna. 'A flower and now a girl,' he whispered, and his eyes were full of joy and wonder. Joanna returned his stare fearfully, but no danger stalked in his eyes, only welcome and intelligence. The giant smiled at her and she was no longer afraid.

9
Nazdarg Number 362d, Rank: Sergeant

Nazdarg number 362d, rank: sergeant, crouched on the floor of his cell and rocked backwards and forwards on his heels as he always did when he was troubled. He was famous in his regiment as one of the first batch to be bred in the 'motherlobes', the artificial wombs that gave birth to his species. He had spent his childhood in Dimrat's House of Many Rooms, but the honour gave him no pleasure. As an adult, he wimpered and cowered at the memory of those days. Dimrat's voice still lacerated his soul and made him bleed inwardly: 'Hello, my little maggot. Look at you! You're ugly and deformed, a beast child. Who would ever want you?'

Nazdarg number 362d remembered when Dimrat had found him playing with the cockroaches that lived under the stairs. 'So you have friends, my little maggot! Shall I show you what daddy does with friends?' Dimrat had picked each cockroach up in turn, crushing them between his finger and thumb. *Splat!* They exploded with a sharp, brittle crack like glass breaking. Afterwards he sat in his hiding place beneath the stairs with the squashed cockroaches lined up in a row at his feet and sobbed until he could sob no more. He had never wept again. He was a beast and beasts have no friends.

But nazdarg number 362d was distressed. Violent changes were taking place in his soul. The dreams had started again. When he was a child, the dreams would always begin in the same way, but the events in each were different. A figure would appear and call out, 'Stephen!' He would run towards the stranger and stop in front of him. The man's skin was darker, much darker than the grey, yet it shone as if it were aflame. 'Who are you? Why have you come?' he would ask, ashamed of his crippled voice, and the stranger would smile at him tenderly and answer: 'I am your father.'

'But I have no father. I am a nazdarg and I come from the motherlobes,' he would reply.

'You were born, my son, before all worlds. I am your true father,' and the stranger would embrace him and his eyes would wash away his doubts like rivers of love.

Later he had asked his father the meaning of the word 'Stephen'. 'It is your name, my son, for so I have called you.'

The dreams were his only relief from the torment of the House of Many Rooms, but they had been silent for twenty years or more. Three weeks earlier, however, he had wakened in the night and seen a figure standing at his feet. 'Who are you?' he had challenged.

'I am your true father.' And as he spoke, the figure turned and light shone in his face—skin darker than the grey, and eyes that cherished him and told him he was worthy to be loved.

Nazdarg number 362d wept. 'It's you,' he whispered. 'You've come back.'

'I've never left you, my son. Never! The hour is near when you will know me as I know you.' Gently, he took the nazdarg's deformed face in both his hands and looked tenderly into his eyes: 'Stephen, this grey and miserable land will soon end. A time of change is here, but do not be afraid. Take this!' His father took his wrist and slipped a bracelet over it. 'When your eyes cannot find me and your heart is tempted to despair, this bracelet will comfort you. It is a token of my love.'

'Father,' croaked nazdarg number 362d, 'you

have never told me your name or where you come from.'

'I have many names and titles, Stephen, but in this land I am called the Captain. As for my home, it is very near and you will share it with me.' And with these words, his father vanished.

When the cold, grey dawn called him from his sleep, he remembered that his father had visited him in the night. Fearful lest it had been an empty dream, he looked at his wrist and saw the bracelet clinging to it. He knew then that he was not a beast but a man, and his true name was Stephen.

Nazdarg number 362d whimpered as he rocked to and fro on his heels. There were thunderings and earthquakes in his soul. His inner world was breaking up: familiar land masses were destroyed, new continents were born, the sky blazed with fire and the oceans roared and foamed. One moment he was a man named Stephen, and in the next, nazdarg number 362d, rank: sergeant, created to serve the will of Dimrat. He reeled over and lay twitching on his face, his fingers tearing at the floor.

After his father's visit, he had been selected to lead the search for Rumbold. The giant's singing still echoed in his mind, the beauty of the melody filling his heart with longing. He was the first to reach the giant after he fell and had seen the tiny flower. He had picked it and hidden it in his water flask. Later, in the privacy of his cell, he had taken out the flower and examined it. It was as light as a snowflake in his hand, yet more beautiful than anything he had ever seen in the world. He did not know the names of the colours, for he had no knowledge of colour, so he named them according to the feelings they gave him. The crimson he called 'warm blood', the blue 'light heart', the green 'sad life', the yellow 'happy one', and the purple he called 'deep rich'.

He had crouched over the flower all night and had

never taken his eyes from it, but as dawn leaked into the high window of his cell, its colours faded and it died.

'The flower has been reborn,' he mumbled. 'I buried the flower and it has risen from the earth a girl.' He had led the patrol that arrested Joanna and had sat behind her during the flight to the castle. He had studied her face, her hair and clothing, and had marvelled that a human could be so beautiful. After he had taken her to the Great Hall of the People, he stood guard at the door, listening, and overheard snatches of conversation: '... I was sent by the Captain to bring colour back to the land.'

Nazdarg number 362d was bewildered: 'Captain' was the name of his father, and the word 'colour' was another way of describing those things which were not grey. Dimrat had created him to obey, to be the servant of his will, but now a new master demanded his allegiance. He lifted his wrist, looked at the bracelet and remembered his true father. The rocking and the whimpering stopped and he sprang upright. He shed his old identity of nazdarg number 362d and became the man Stephen. He had made his decision. It was nazdarg number 362d who had consigned the giant and the girl to the cage, but it was the man Stephen who must release them. Dimrat would be cheated of his prey.

Stephen limped along the passage to the serum room. The nazdargs, on rare occasions, had fits of madness in which their human part would awake and shake the bars of the cage that held them. At such times, they were injected with a serum that rendered them unconscious for three days.

Stephen paused outside the door and listened. Silence! As sergeant of the nazdargs, he was the keeper of the keys. He opened the door and slid inside. The darkness hung around him like a fog, but he knew where the syringes and the serum were kept. He picked them up and closed the door behind him. Loading a syringe with serum, he quietly opened the door of the first cell. Nazdarg number 72110L, rank: foot soldier, was curled on the floor snoring. One eye was open, but it was blind with sleep. Stephen leaned across the nazdarg's body and injected the serum into his arm. The foot soldier stirred and his other eye opened, but it was blank and uncomprehending. In less than an hour, the castle's regiment of nazdargs was immobilised. Stephen returned the used syringes and the empty serum bottles to the room and went in search of Crispian.

There were few to be trusted in the castle, but Crispian was the exception. He was the only remaining descendant of the old kings—a short, strongly-built man who made no secret of his contempt for the government. Dimrat permitted him to be free but gave him no power. It was Dimrat's greatest cruelty. Crispian was forced to witness the ruin of his country and people and could do nothing about it. He was a good man and would have made a capable and wise leader, but his impotence was slowly eating him up. During the long years of Dimrat's rule, hope had fled his life, leaving nothing but a deep cavity filled with despair. It was only Crispian's rage and the love of his wife that kept him alive.

Stephen needed Crispian if the giant and the girl were to escape. The nazdarg's spirit had been broken in childhood and recreated to obey Dimrat's will without question. He had rebelled against his master, but he needed an ally, someone with the experience and wisdom to guide him. Moreover, Crispian's wife was the only person in all the castle who had ever smiled and greeted him as if he mattered.

He knocked gently on the door and waited. It opened and he slid inside.

10

The Cage

'My name is Rumbold. What's your name?' inquired the giant.

'Joanna, Joanna Bradley.' Joanna liked the giant instantly. He was unwashed and his clothes were stained and torn, but he had a nobility that his circumstances could not hide. She could see the huge slabs of muscle on his upper chest and thighs and could feel energy radiating from him like electricity, yet she felt safe and relaxed in his company. When least expecting it, Joanna had found a friend.

'I'm sorry if I embarrassed you with my staring, but you are the only person I've ever seen who's retained her colour. Looking at you is like looking through a window at the land before the grey smothered it. It reminds me of what we've lost. Where do you come from? Why are you here?'

'I come from Britain.'

'Where?'

'Britain—an island in the northern hemisphere. It's part of the European continent.'

'My mother told me about Europe. But what of your reason for being here?'

'The Captain sent me.' Joanna told the giant her story, relieved to find a person who believed in colour. He listened in silence, never interrupting her, and Joanna was reassured by his presence. His eyes were gentle and intelligent, and his face was so sensitive that it expressed every change of feeling.

Only when Joanna had finished her story did Rumbold question her: 'Tell me more about the Captain. My mother told me that the Captain had come to my ceremony of naming, but I have no memory of it. My mother loved him and said that he would return and save the land, but I thought it was another of her dreams. I trusted in my strength and weapons—not in the Captain. I reasoned that if he couldn't stop the grey when it first crept across the land, he wouldn't have the power to remove it later.'

'The Captain's a mystery man. He doesn't make sense. When you're with him, you know that he's absolutely good and would never tell a lie or deceive you. He's also powerful, frighteningly powerful. In comparison, Dimrat and your president are a couple of wimps. When you meet him, he's so alive and healthy that he's scary. You don't want him to go away, but you're afraid that if he comes too close you won't be able to bear it. His eyes are beautiful and terrible at the same time. When I say "terrible", I don't mean wicked or evil, but they're like a beam of light. In my country, if a ray of light penetrates a dark and neglected room, all the particles of dust in its path show up. The Captain's eyes are like that. When he looks at you, he looks right inside you and makes you see parts of yourself that you'd rather keep hidden.'

'I always thought that if the Captain existed, he'd be exactly as you described him. Why doesn't he make sense?'

'When I'm with him, I know that he is good and he loves me. He also has the power to do anything.' Joanna groped for words to describe her struggle.

'Go on,' encouraged Rumbold.

'I'll try but I'm very confused. Although my heart tells me that he's okay, my experience denies it. Why did he allow Dimrat to throw me from the airship? Why did he run away at the end of the concert and leave me to be captured by those creatures? Why am I here in this cage? I feel ripped off. When you look into his eyes, you can't help yourself: you trust him and you forget your doubts—they seem stupid—but when you're in a mess and need him desperately, he's not around to help, or doesn't seem to be. I can try and make sense of it by saying he's attempting to teach me something, but it's not a very good excuse: Hey folks, I've been beaten up, stoned, screamed and jeered at, imprisoned and almost killed, and do you know why? Because the good Captain loves me and wants to teach me an important lesson! It's not a very convincing argument, is it? If my dad knew I was in a fix, I think he'd give up his own life to save me. He wouldn't run away.'

Joanna looked intently into the giant's face, her eyes pleading for answers, but there was no response. For a moment, he had forgotten her, forgotten everything, and was wandering in the forbidden country of the past. The memories haunted him like vengeful ghosts. Misery! Remorse! Rage! Sadness! Guilt! Crushing, relentless guilt! His eyes bled like open wounds and his body trembled.

Joanna forgot about herself. 'Are you okay?' she inquired urgently. 'Did I say something that upset you? I'm sorry if I did.'

The giant's eyes cleared, but they were still full of pain. 'I'm all right. No, it wasn't your fault. I'd like to meet your Captain and ask him some questions myself one day.'

'You looked awful, Rumbold. What was wrong with you?'

The giant silenced her question with his eyes.

'Oh, I'm sorry, I didn't mean to pry.'

Rumbold smiled at her and the pain was driven from his eyes. 'You weren't to know, Joanna. You meant well.'

To hide her embarrassment, and because she could think of nothing better to say, she slipped her backpack off her shoulders and opened the side pocket: 'Would you like a piece of chocolate?'

'I beg your pardon?'

Joanna laughed. 'Chocolate is something that you eat. It's made with milk and cocoa beans and tastes fantastic. The Captain gave me it.'

'Yes please.'

Joanna gave him a large slab of chocolate and watched him as he ate it.

'Delicious! Your friend the Captain may leave you in some tight spots, but he provides you with excellent food. What does he look like?'

'His hair is short cropped and curly and his skin is black.'

'Black?'

'Sorry! I forgot that you have no knowledge of colour. His skin is the same colour as my hair.'

The giant grew thoughtful. 'I think I've met your Captain; not in person but in a dream. If he is the same, I cannot believe that he wishes any evil to befall you.'

A large thrush flew down and sat on a bar above them.

'Look!' cried Joanna. 'That's the first bird I've seen in this horrible land, and I think he's watching us.'

The thrush sang, the sweet, clear notes ringing in the air about them like an orchestra of tiny bells, and as it sang, grey plumage turned mottled brown and its grey beak caught fire and burned like a flickering yellow flame. Fluttering down, it perched on Joanna's hand, put its head to one side and looked at her steadily with bright, black eyes. The pulley wheels squealed and the cage began to move slowly downwards.

At the first shudder of movement, the thrush launched itself from Joanna's hand and flew away, but its song still lingered, replayed by the echoes until they too took wing and flew out across the night.

'I'm chained to the floor and can't look down. What's happening?'

'Nothing!' responded Joanna. 'I can see nothing.' But as she spoke a figure strode from the shelter of

the wall and looked upwards. Crispian had heard the
thrush's song and knew it for a sign.

'The land will be reborn,' he whispered, and for
the first time in many years hope kindled and blazed
in his heart.

11

Escape

The cage touched the ground with a jolt and a muffled
crash. At any other time the sound would have been
inaudible, but in the night, it was amplified by the
silence. The figure stood alert for several seconds,
scanning the windows and doors of the castle for any
sign of alarm. When he was satisfied that no one had
been disturbed, he walked quickly to the cage and
unlocked it. Slowly, to avoid the squeal of rusty
hinges, he opened the cage door and stepped inside,
lifting a finger to his lips in warning.

'Please be quiet,' he whispered. 'My name's
Crispian and I'm a descendant of the true king. I'll
explain later. Don't be afraid. I've come to rescue you.'

A second figure approached, moving as silently as
a shadow. He ran with a slight limp and his body
was huge and misshapen. Joanna recognised him.
'We're discovered,' she whispered urgently. 'It's the
leader of those beast-men that captured me.'

'The nazdarg's a friend. If it wasn't for him, there'd
be no escape. You'd be vivisected in Dimrat's
laboratories,' said Crispian. 'Now be quiet or your
voices will betray us.'

The nazdarg ran on all fours like an ape, his huge

arms assisting his legs and propelling him forward with incredible speed. His grotesque appearance belied his agility and strength. He swept towards them like a landslide, leapt the final ten metres and landed soundlessly in the interior of the cage. He looked uncertainly at them and gathered his arms around him protectively, cringing before the battery of their eyes, fearing rejection.

Rumbold's face lit up. He ignored the request for silence and greeted the nazdarg: 'Thank you, brother,' and stretched his manacled hands towards him in greeting. The nazdarg was confused and tears shone in his eyes. No one had ever called him 'brother'. He undid Rumbold's chains and then cowered in the corner, afraid that the giant would turn on him and beat him. Rumbold's face was full of compassion. 'We are true brothers,' he whispered reassuringly.

'How can we be brothers?' asked the nazdarg, the words falling from his lips in broken fragments.

Rumbold took the nazdarg in his arms and spoke quietly to him. The nazdarg's body stiffened and the ridge of hair that stretched along his spine bristled with tension. Suddenly the tension snapped and he cast his great arms about the body of the giant. The nazdarg had found his brother.

'Leave your reunion for later and follow me,' commanded Crispian.

Joanna and Rumbold followed their rescuers across the courtyard to the kitchen door. Crispian opened it, turned and signalled to the company to follow.

Joanna kept close to Rumbold, amazed by his size. He was at least twelve feet tall, but fortunately the ceilings in the castle were high and he could walk without difficulty. Rumbold was not awkward or clumsy, but moved with the grace of a dancer, his feet whispering across the floor like a giant cat's.

They raced through the kitchen, along a twisting passageway, and up a narrow flight of stone stairs.

Voices disturbed them. The nazdarg detached himself from the party and sped on ahead. There was a series of stifled cries and thuds and the voices were heard no more. The nazdarg returned and beckoned to them to follow.

The stairway opened into a wide hall, and scattered across it were the sprawled bodies of an elite guard of secret police. Their revolvers were only half drawn from their holsters, giving the impression that they had suddenly fallen asleep on duty.

Rumbold grinned at the nazdarg: 'I suppose you gave them a sleeping pill each for their insomnia!' Before the nazdarg could reply, the giant leapt into the air, somersaulted and lashed out with his foot. There was a sharp crack followed by the clatter of a weapon. A guard had feigned unconsciousness, risen to one knee and levelled his revolver at the nazdarg's back. In the fraction of a second before the gun detonated, Rumbold's foot smashed into his jaw.

The party froze, the clatter of the weapon echoing around them, multiplying in volume until it seemed to fill the castle, but no alarm rang out. Silence stalked into the hall on soft padded paws and killed the last of the echoes. The party relaxed and let out their breath in the same instant.

'That was a close thing,' gasped Crispian. 'We need to hide those bodies before they're discovered. As soon as they're found, the alarm will sound and the chase will begin in earnest.'

'Kill them,' counselled the nazdarg. 'They're scum. They kill and torture for the joy of it. And anyway, dead man don't talk. I'll finish the job I started and break their necks.' His hands mimed the action.

'There'll be no killing,' said Crispian. 'We'll gag them, tie them up and lock them in a room.'

'But they're evil. Their trade is death and torture. They deserve to die. We'll never be safe if they're alive,' protested the nazdarg.

'They're still men, and we have no right to take their lives. If we kill them when they're defenceless, we're no better than they are, Stephen. Where can we hide them?'

The nazdarg growled and locked eyes with Crispian.

Rumbold placed his hand gently on the nazdarg's arm. 'He's right, brother. Life is a precious gift and we have no authority to take it. Killing the guards will only resurrect the beast within you and destroy your human likeness. That's what Dimrat wants. Don't let him win.'

The nazdarg shrugged his shoulders. 'Have it your own way,' he said, 'but if you let them live, they'll kill again.'

'If death is your answer to evil men, where will you stop?' asked Crispian. 'You'll flood the world with blood and drown both the good and the evil. You'll begin by killing murderers like the elite guard, and when killing becomes easy, the hungry child for stealing bread, the cripple for walking too slowly. You of all men know this to be true. Kill and a little of your human soul will die as well. Let me ask you again: where can we hide the guards?'

'Over there,' he replied grudgingly, pointing to the far corner of the hall, and suddenly relief swamped his soul. He tried to speak but he was dumb. Stephen killed because he loathed himself; death was the measure of his self-hatred. But in that moment he saw the truth, not clearly, but like a distant country seen through a bank of fog: if he killed the guards it would be defeat; to let them live was victory. His relief was quickly followed by a new emotion: compassion for all living things. This was his father's world and he must care for it.

He found his voice again: 'A nazdarg foot soldier's asleep in that cell. He's drugged and won't wake up for a long time. The guards will be safe with him.' Stephen's eyes were bright, and he touched his lips in wonder. He could speak without stuttering; his fractured words were mended.

'Take the bodies,' commanded Crispian, 'and hide them in the cell.' The giant and the nazdarg lifted up the eight men, two under each arm, and carried them to the cell.

Crispian turned and smiled at Joanna. 'Those two were created to kill. I would never have believed that either of them would have obeyed me and let the guards live. A miracle has taken place. Four weeks ago Rumbold wiped out a gunship patrol and an entire battalion of infantry. There were no survivors. The president launched the biggest manhunt in the history of his government to capture him. Now, for some unknown reason, the giant has turned pacifist and the nazdarg allows me to talk him out of killing the guards. Did you see his face when he agreed to spare them?' Before Joanna could reply, he answered the question himself: 'He seemed relieved and his eyes were full of gladness. I thought he was going to hug me.' He was still smiling when Rumbold and Stephen returned.

'Follow me!' commanded Crispian, and he proceeded to lead them through a labyrinth of passages and rooms until they came to a short staircase that ended at a door. Crispian tapped on it twice and waited. The door swung silently open, revealing the slender figure of a woman. Even the dull grey of her skin and clothing could not hide her beauty. 'Welcome!' she said warmly, and she invited them to enter with a graceful gesture of her hand.

As the nazdarg was about to pass through the door, the woman placed her hands gently on his chest and restrained him. 'Thank you, Stephen,' she whispered. 'I always knew that the man in you would triumph in the end.' And she stood on tiptoe and kissed him on the lips. 'The Captain will reward you with a great happiness and you will forget the misery of the past.'

Joanna entered the room with Rumbold. 'So, the two caged birds have flown away together,' said the woman, and she took their hands in hers. 'My name is Martha, and Crispian is my husband. You are both welcome in our home. Come!' She put her arm about Joanna's waist and drew her into the room.

'It's not safe for us to stay here,' said Crispian, 'but this castle contains secrets that even Dimrat and the president are ignorant of. Come this way!'

He led them through several large rooms into a library. The dry, musky smell of books still clung to the room, but the shelves were empty and covered in a light snowfall of dust. Crispian walked briskly to a large writing desk, pulled out a side drawer and inserted his hand.

'There!' he said and swung round to face the party. 'Look!' They followed the direction of his gaze and gasped. The entire wall rose vertically into the ceiling, revealing an exact duplicate of the library. But what a difference! The shelves were loaded with books, pictures hung on the walls and, best of all, the room retained its colours. Martha took Crispian by the hand and led him into their secret kingdom. The grey shroud vanished and they stood before the party transformed, swathed in splendid colours. Crispian was swarthy with dark, haunted eyes and hollow cheeks, and, in contrast, Martha was tall and shapely, with a strong, tender face, chestnut hair and frank, grey-green eyes, the colour of a winter sea.

She smiled. 'Come!' she said. 'We have prepared a surprise for our guests.'

Stephen and Rumbold sprang into the library together, but Joanna held back. 'It's like being in a cinema,' she thought. 'Everything's dark and grey except the screen.'

The room made very little difference to Rumbold. His skin remained the colour of grey stone, but it glistened as if oil had been poured over it. Stephen, however, changed instantly. The grey fell from his deformed body and he glowed with colour. His skin was a soft brown, and the hair on his spine was the rich gold of ripened corn.

He turned and looked at Joanna, and his eyes were the colour of an evening sky: a dark, mystic blue. Joanna was shaken. 'He has the Captain's eyes,' she thought, 'but they've been copied in a different colour.'

'Come,' said Martha, 'and see the feast we've prepared for you.'

Joanna stepped into the library and the wall closed noiselessly behind her. Here she would learn the secrets of the country's past and be guided in her quest.

She wriggled out of her backpack and followed the party to the dining room.

12

Dinner

For the first time since her arrival in the grey land, Joanna felt safe. She had lived with the threat of danger in Brixton and was beginning to adapt to her new circumstances. Moreover she was no longer alone, but supported by four companions. She moved swiftly after Martha and caught her before she reached the dining room door.

'Could I wash my hands and face before I eat?' she requested. 'I'll probably die of food poisoning if I eat like this.' She lifted her hands, palms upwards, and showed them to Martha.

'Oh, I am sorry,' said the older woman, and she turned to the other members of the party. 'Would you like to wash before you eat?'

Rumbold gave his wry half smile. 'Wash! I need a bath, but I don't suppose you have one to fit me. And look at my clothes! I've worn them for seven weeks.'

'Only seven weeks?' said Martha, returning his smile. 'I'll soak them in disinfectant and wash them for you, and Crispian can repair the tears.'

'And how about a bath?'

'You're lucky. Our bath is designed for two, so you'll fit.' Martha wrinkled her nose in mock disgust. 'You'll be better company afterwards. We don't have any clothes that will fit you, but I think we can provide a blanket that'll serve as a kilt.'

Joanna washed her hands and face and combed her hair. She admired her face in the mirror, adopting her most adult expression: lips pouted and her dark eyes staring back at her mysteriously, hiding their secrets. She laughed and chided her reflection: 'You're no ugly sister, Cinderella, but you're very vain,' and she flicked a tiny globule of foam onto her nose as a penance. When she laughed, the suave image in the mirror vanished and she was a girl again: bright eyes with a smile that lit her face.

Rumbold put his head round the door. 'This is not a beauty salon, Joanna. You're pretty enough without having to confirm it in a mirror. If you don't leave soon and let me bath, I'll suffocate on my own body odour.'

Joanna smiled at him cheekily. 'Patience! Just hold your breath for a couple of minutes.'

'It's hard to be patient when a feast is waiting for me in the dining room. I haven't eaten properly for nine days.'

Joanna was suddenly concerned. 'I'm sorry! I had no idea you were so hungry.' And then she looked up at him and saw the width of his shoulders and the power of his body. 'If you're undernourished, what do you look like after a few good meals?'

'Like this,' said Rumbold, and he lifted her playfully above his head with one hand.

'Put me down or I'll kick you.'

'You put it so nicely,' said Rumbold, 'that I can't possibly refuse.' He lowered her in one swift movement and placed her outside the bathroom door, closing it before she had time to re-enter.

Joanna was still smiling when Martha found her.

'You look happy, Joanna. What's up?'

'Oh, nothing! Nothing!'

'It is rare that "nothing" makes a young woman smile,' she said. Her green eyes were as sharp as diamonds. 'Come with me and we'll have a drink while we're waiting for the others to arrive. Would you like fruit juice or coffee?'

'A fruit juice, please.'

The meal was sumptuous. The centre-piece of the table was a huge joint of meat glazed with butter and decorated with bright red cherries. Arranged around it was a variety of fowl and vegetable dishes: mallards cooked in wine and stuffed with apricots, breast of chicken curried in spices and topped with fresh cream, roast quail and pheasant, plantains fried in butter, succulent baby carrots, pilau rice, sweet yams, crisp golden corn and peppers stuffed with nuts and mushrooms.

Rumbold sat at the head of the table, sampling the food with his eyes and nose like a connoisseur. 'My congratulations on a splendid meal,' he said, and he looked appreciatively at Martha.

'Don't look at me, Rumbold. Crispian's the chef. He prepared the dishes and I merely kept them warm for you.'

'Thank you, Crispian. It is rare for a king to serve his subjects.'

Crispian's face grew sad and the meal lost its

joviality. 'A king, Rumbold? A king without a throne! A king without subjects! Yes, I am the last descendant of the true king, but my crown is worn by Dimrat and the president wields my sceptre. They permit me to live and provide a generous allowance. Why? So they can taunt me with my powerlessness! "Crispian," they say, "we're going to introduce a policy of infanticide and kill unwanted children. What is your opinion?" And when I protest and cry for justice, they laugh and clap their hands in mockery. What sort of king am I, Rumbold? A king in chains! A king of fools! A jester to the court of Dimrat! When the pain of living becomes too great, I long for death. But I cannot betray my people. While they suffer, I must live and trust in the mercy of the Captain. You say it's rare for a king to serve his subjects? Oh that the people of this land could gather at my table: the rich and poor, the noble and the lowly. I would be a humble king and serve them joyfully.'

Rumbold looked at Crispian steadily and then knelt before him. 'I will be the servant of the servant king.'

'This is not a time for speeches, Crispian,' said Martha, and her voice was warm but chiding. 'You'll have us all bowing and scraping and swearing allegiance to you. Remember, we're here to eat! Do you want to serve your four loyal subjects cold food? It's hardly an auspicious beginning to your reign: Hail, king of the cold table!'

'Forgive me,' said Crispian, and smiled at the company self-consciously. 'I'm not a very good servant. I should have been thinking of your welfare and . . .'

'Not another speech, my love. Spare us! Please begin.' Martha caressed her husband's face with her fingertips and then turned to the guests. 'Eat! Rumbold, you look famished. Eat as much as you like. Stephen, you're an honoured guest. We're delighted to have you at our table. I've heard that nazdargs have enormous appetites. Eat! And you, Joanna. You look as if you need to put on a little weight. Good home cooking is what you need. Help yourself and don't be shy.'

Joanna needed very little encouragement. She had not eaten for twenty-four hours and was very hungry. Crispian's speech had depressed her, but the delicious aroma and taste of the food restored her humour. Soon, however, the demands of her appetite became less insistent and her curiosity returned. She studied Crispian's face and became aware of the rage and frustration that gnawed at his soul. Here sat a great and noble man: a caged lion doomed to pace his cage and glare and growl at his tormentors.

'Excuse me,' she said, addressing herself to him, 'but would you mind answering some questions?'

13

Discussion

Crispian nodded, his own pain forgotten in his concern for Joanna. 'I'll try,' he said and smiled, the appeal of his eyes so powerful that she longed to win his approval.

'I was sent to this land by the Captain and . . .'

'The Captain?' said Crispian in astonishment. 'Do you mean *the* Captain?'

'I suppose so. I don't know of any other Captain who'd fly me halfway round the world in his airship, and then ask me to bring colour back to a grey land. I can't tell you much about him. We've only met on a couple of occasions.'

'The Captain sent *you*?'

'Yes! What's wrong with me?'

'Nothing! But you're not quite the champion we were expecting. You're just a young girl—hardly an expert in war and military tactics.'

'Just a young girl!' echoed Joanna angrily. 'I might be "just a young girl" to you, but this girl is sixteen years of age and can look after herself.' She was tempted to tell him of the school prizes she'd won and her recent success in the British karate championships, but she bit her lip and was content to scowl at him.

Martha came to her rescue. 'She may be "just a girl", Crispian, but the Captain knows what he's doing. A girl sent by the Captain is better than an army without him.'

'I wish the Captain wasn't so unpredictable. And what of the prophecy? He said that a saviour would come out of the west and restore colour to the land. He said a "saviour" and not a teenage girl. We need a man of action, a man of experience and maturity. We'd never be able to start a revolt with this girl. Imagine what the people would say if I presented Joanna as the promised saviour? I'd never be taken seriously again.'

'She's very brave,' said Stephen.

'How do you know?'

'I was listening outside the government hall door. She threw the deputy on his back for hitting her and stood up to the president.'

'This discussion is getting us nowhere,' said Rumbold. 'I don't claim to know much about the Captain, but the fact remains that Joanna has been sent to restore colour to the land. How else can we explain her presence and the colour of her skin and clothes? If you don't think she's suitable, your quarrel's with him. My counsel is that we trust the wisdom of the Captain. She may be "just a girl", but she's the Captain's girl and that's good enough for me.'

'I'm sorry,' said Crispian. 'You're right, of course, but why does the Captain always do the unexpected?'

'Because he is the Captain,' replied Martha.

Crispian smiled apologetically at Joanna, but disappointment still lurked in his eyes. 'I'm sorry for what I said. When we rescued you, we had no idea that the Captain had sent you.'

'Why did you do it?'

'Because you retained your colour and we didn't want you to be taken to Dimrat's House of Many Rooms. Stephen knew the torment you'd suffer and pleaded with me to help you escape. Did the Captain give you any instructions?'

'No. He told me what he wanted me to do, but gave me no guidance. I don't know why your land has turned grey and I have no idea how to bring the colours back to it. I feel like someone who's been given a spoon and told to empty the ocean.'

'Dimrat's sorcery has turned the country grey,' said Crispian. Rage drove the disappointment from his eyes. 'How much do you know of Dimrat?'

'Very little! I dreamed of his exile from the land, and he's tried to murder me on a couple of occasions, but I don't know anything about him.'

'Yes, he was exiled, but he returned in disguise.'

'Why did you send him away? What was his crime?'

'My father was the king, and Dimrat was his friend from boyhood: a man of genius and a natural leader. He and his sister were both members of the government.'

'Dimrat has a sister?'

'He had a sister, but she vanished. There are rumours. Some say that Dimrat murdered her, and others that she fled across the sea and found refuge. Adriana was Dimrat's identical twin, but she didn't resemble him in character. She shared her brother's genius, but not his pride.'

'What was she like?'

'Martha will tell you. She's her daughter.'

'Her daughter!' exclaimed Joanna in surprise.

'Yes, I'm her daughter. My mother was brilliant like her brother, but she was resented for her outspokenness. She spent her life fighting prejudice. Dimrat was charming, but the battles scarred my mother and made her sharp-tongued and aggressive. She was a fighter, but hidden beneath her armour was a kind and honourable woman. It was my mother who first exposed Dimrat.'

Crispian took up the story again: 'Dimrat was a geneticist. He did excellent work on hereditary diseases and was acclaimed throughout the country. But his genius was his downfall. He despised people who were less intelligent than he was, and he believed that human beings were incapable of governing themselves. He dreamed of a new world in which human weakness would be ruthlessly repressed. The dream obsessed him, and in secret he created his own private army and planned to overthrow the government.'

'What do you mean by, "he created his own private army"?' asked Joanna.

Martha answered the question: 'He created human life artificially. Rumbold and Stephen are both results of his genetic experiments. He approached my mother and asked for her assistance, but she was disgusted by his work. She attempted to expose him, but no one believed her. As far as the government and public were concerned, she was a jealous sister making trouble for the nation's darling. He'd been nominated for a Nobel prize, you see.'

'How was he exposed then?'

'The giants exposed him,' replied Martha.

'The giants!' exclaimed Joanna, and she turned and looked at Rumbold. But Rumbold's head was lowered and his eyes were hidden from her view.

'Yes, we exposed him,' said Rumbold. 'We escaped from his House of Many Rooms and told the nation that he'd created us to overthrow the government. Adriana was vindicated and Dimrat was exiled for the crime of treason.'

'But he returned,' said Crispian, 'determined to wreak revenge on my father and fulfil his dream of a new world. Before his exile, Dimrat was supported by a group of fellow-conspirators. Their identities were never discovered. On his return, he gathered them together and planned the overthrow of the government. Foremost among them was the president. Dimrat resumed his genetic experiments and created the nazdarg legions and the death squads.'

'What are the death squads?' The name sent a chill of fear through Joanna.

'They are human beings like you and me, but Dimrat operated on their brains and turned them into zombies. Hundreds died in the early days of his experiments, but he finally perfected the process. They are his most deadly weapons. A death squad commando has no free will but blindly obeys the orders of Dimrat. It was a suicide death squad that assassinated my father and his cabinet. They shot their way into the senate building, murdered my father and his colleagues and then turned their weapons on themselves.'

Joanna's face was aghast. 'Why weren't Dimrat and the other conspirators arrested?'

'The murder of my father was a brilliant coup. The president was the Chief of Security and so was responsible for the enquiry into his death. Acting on the instructions of Dimrat, he used the opportunity to arrest all the politicians who were loyal to my father and accuse them of treason. Any voice that was lifted in protest was silenced. The death squads saw to that.'

'Wasn't there a public outcry? Didn't the people riot and strike?'

'There were protests, and the media tried to investigate my father's death, but any journalist who blundered too near the truth simply disappeared. Moreover, the president won the support of the people by promising them Utopia.'

'Utopia?'

'A perfect world.' Crispian had already forgotten that he was answering Joanna's questions and he addressed his answers to the whole company. 'He's always been the arch-manipulator. Dimrat despises people, but the president understands their value. He knew that the people were basically selfish, so he bribed them with wealth and luxury goods and they quickly forgot their principles. People are often more willing to listen to their greed than to their conscience. Is that true in your country?'

'I suppose it is. I've never really thought about it. But how did the people react when the world turned grey?'

'It happened so gradually that people hardly noticed. The president diverted their attention by filling their pockets with money and their heads with dreams of earthly paradise. He turned the land into a vast shopping mall and drove the people crazy with desire. He controlled the banks and offered unlimited credit, achieving what no other dictator had ever done before: total power over the population and the ability to recreate the world in any way he chose. Greed blinded the people and they hardly noticed the colours fading from the land. When the grey finally shrouded the land, it was an easy matter for the president to convince the people that colour had never existed. Those who protested were sent to Dimrat's laboratories for re-education.'

'Didn't anyone try to stop the grey from spreading across the land?'

'Certainly, but all attempts were futile. Nobody knew where the grey came from.'

'Nobody?'

'My mother knew,' said Martha, 'but she fled the land.'

'It's more likely that she's dead, my love,' said Crispian gently. 'She vanished on the night of my father's murder.'

'I know she's not dead. She's alive. I know in my heart that she's alive.'

'Surely you can't believe the rumours?'

'I do, Crispian. The outlaws may be brigands and poorly educated, but they're free and continue to fight against Dimrat. What possible gain could they achieve by inventing such a story?'

'They're superstitious. If I remember correctly, the story goes something like this: a woman called Adriana was carried by angels to the shore of the sea. She lived with the outlaws for several days, and then turned into a fish and vanished into the ocean. It doesn't sound very credible, does it?'

'Dimrat believes the story. At least, he believes that his sister lives.' Stephen had been silent during the discussion, but now he spoke for the first time.

'Adriana's alive.'

'How do you know?' demanded Crispian.

'Because I led the nazdarg patrol that was charged with the responsibility of finding her. She escaped after the murder of your father and fled eastwards. We followed her scent across the deadlands but it ended abruptly in a shallow basin of sand. It disappeared as if a giant hand had lifted her out of the world. In those days, the president's spies had infiltrated the outlaw bands. We were told she had reappeared again. The message was garbled but the gist of it was that two men had flown with her from the sky—I think that's where the angel myth comes from—and a third joined her shortly afterwards. He was well known to the outlaws, and at his direction they gave Adriana hospitality. We arrived four days after receiving the message, but Adriana had gone. We . . .'

'Go on,' encouraged Crispian, but Stephen's eyes were troubled and his speech, which until that moment had been fluent, was reduced to a stutter, petering off into a silence.

'We . . . I . . . captured . . . outlaws . . . tort . . .'

Rumbold came swiftly to his assistance: 'You captured the outlaws and interrogated them?' Stephen nodded dumbly and his blue eyes were full of remorse. 'Did they tell you where she'd gone?' Stephen nodded again and his lips moved as if he was trying to pronounce words, but they were all prisoners, barred from escape by the cage of his guilt.

'The past is the past,' said Martha, and she took Stephen's hand in her own. 'The nazdarg is dead. Long live the man!'

Stephen turned towards Martha gratefully. His lips moved in a desperate attempt to speak and suddenly the bars broke and the prisoners fled their cage: 'Several of the outlaws escaped, but we killed most of them. It was a child, a girl, who told us the story. A man she referred to as the "Captain" called a school of dolphins and commanded them to take Adriana to safety across the sea.'

'Where can we find the girl?' asked Crispian.

'She is dead,' said Stephen, and his eyes were full of guilt and regret. 'There are other survivors. If we can locate the outlaw bands, we may find someone who can tell us of her whereabouts. They're hunted by the death squads and the nazdarg legions, but they've eluded capture. If you want to find Adriana, you'll have to find the outlaws first.'

'That's impossible,' said Crispian. 'You're safe in this secret apartment, but once you leave, the death squad gunships will hunt you down. The president chose the location of his headquarters very carefully.

This castle is in the centre of a plain. There are no shrubs or trees that will serve as cover. Once you leave, you'll be visible for miles.'

'They could go in our car,' said Martha hopefully.

'A car is no match for a gunship, even an E-Type Jaguar like ours,' responded Crispian, and he looked into the face of each of his guests in turn. 'It would only make you a bigger target for a missile.'

'We could always put the gunships out of action,' said Joanna.

'And how do you intend to do that?' said Crispian, curiously. His tone suggested that she was interfering and should mind her own business.

Joanna desperately wanted to win the acceptance of Crispian, but she was also angry with him. 'As far as he's concerned,' she thought, 'I'm just a kid; a nobody. I'll show him.' Her eyes switched to combative mode and she stalked Crispian pitilessly. 'What sort of gunships are they anyway?'

'What do you mean, "What sort of gunships?",' he blustered.

'Are they powered by the old type of piston engine or by a shaft turbine engine? My dad flew Westland Silkorsky Sea Kings and Lynxes for the Royal Navy. I may be just a "young girl" to you, Crispian, but I know enough to put the gunships out of action.'

Crispian had the look of a man who had just put his finger into a bird cage and his pet canary had bitten it off. 'I don't rightly know,' he said lamely, 'but I suppose we could set them on fire.'

'You don't rightly know,' said Joanna ironically, 'so you decide to play games with matches. Do you want martyrdom?'

'I beg your pardon?'

'Do you want to be a martyr?'

'I don't know what you mean.'

'I'll explain it to you. Aviation fuel is one of the most volatile and inflammable substances on earth.

If you "light a little bonfire" under the gunships you'll be incinerated. It's a very dramatic way to die, a fitting funeral pyre for the last descendant of the king. There are far more sensible ways to immobilise a gunship. I'll do it for you.'

'But it's very dangerous. I'd feel terrible sending a young girl like you to destroy the gunships. This is a job for an experienced saboteur.'

'Give me a break!' said Joanna angrily. 'If the Captain thought it was okay to send me to help bring back the colours to the land, he was hardly trying to protect me from danger.'

'She's right, Crispian,' said Martha firmly, but laughter brimmed in her eyes.

'If you're worried, I'll act as her minder,' volunteered Rumbold, 'and see that she returns safely.'

Joanna was beginning to regret both her rudeness to Crispian and her offer to help sabotage the gunships. The nearest she had ever come to an engine was when she had helped service her father's car, but she was too proud to admit ignorance. 'We'll have to act quickly,' she said, 'and make the most of the final minutes of darkness. Dawn can't be far off.' She turned to Crispian uncertainly. 'I'm sorry that I was so rude to you.'

'He deserved it,' said Martha, and then she began to laugh. 'Sometimes, my love, you take yourself too seriously. You're a king and one day you'll reign over this land, but you're also very human and that's one of the reasons why I love you so much.'

Crispian looked at Joanna properly for the first time and there was respect in his eyes. 'Will you accept my apology?'

'Yes, if you accept my apology for being so rude to you.'

'It's a deal,' said Crispian, and from that moment they became friends.

Joanna and Rumbold slid silently into the court-yard. Already the sky was brightening and soon the sun would spill a torrent of grey light across the land. The gunships stood in a row, their blades folded across their fuselages like the wings of giant insects. 'It seems deserted,' whispered Rumbold, 'but I'll scout round and make sure. You start work on the nearest gunship.'

Joanna was about to swing herself into the cabin of the gunship when an instinct made her turn. A death squad commando stood behind her and his gun was levelled at her head.

14

The Flight

As she turned, Joanna saw surprise in the commando's dull eyes. She reacted instantly. The movements were choreographed like the steps of a dancer, but faster and more deadly, rehearsed in countless training sessions and demonstration bouts. Her left foot moved upwards in a blur of speed and crashed into the commando's head, hurling him backwards. With the reflexes of a trained karate fighter, Joanna regained her balance and caught the revolver before it clattered to the ground.

A sound startled her. She swung round, pirouetting on her toes, her body transformed into a weapon. 'Keep your feet to yourself, young lady,' whispered Rumbold, and there was a chuckle in his voice. 'That was very nicely done. He'll have a very bad case of memory loss when he wakes up, and even if he doesn't, he'll choose not to remember the incident.'

'What do you mean?' hissed Joanna.

'He'll never be able to admit to his death squad pals that he was beaten by a child.' Rumbold evaded the savage kick that was aimed at his shin and then lifted his hands in a gesture of mock surrender. 'That was a superb display of the martial arts, Joanna. I've seldom seen a better kick. Let's gag this commando and tie him up, and then we'll get to work.'

Joanna looked glumly at Rumbold and was unable to meet his eyes. Rumbold studied her face for a few seconds and then smiled. 'I think the girl knows more about karate than gunships. Remind me! Who was it who asked the question: Are they powered by the old type of piston engine or by a shaft turbine engine?'

'But Crispian was treating me like a child,' protested Joanna. 'That "daddy knows best" voice he used drove me crazy.'

'Did your father really fly Westland Silkorsky Sea Kings and Lynxes?'

'No! He gets dizzy on a step ladder. My dad's a butcher.'

'You mean that you've duped Crispian into thinking that you're some kind of wizard with aero-engines, and you know nothing about them whatsoever?'

'Yeah!'

'How did you expect to sabotage them?'

'I was going to improvise.'

'I can see that you're very good at that sort of thing,' retorted Rumbold sharply.

'You have to be if you want to survive on the streets of Brixton.'

'Survive! After what I saw you do to that death squad commando, it's not your survival that I'm worried about.'

Joanna looked bleakly into the face of Rumbold. 'Forgive me for getting you into this mess. I was too proud to take all that baby talk.'

'Stay here and keep watch. I'll sabotage the gunships,' said Rumbold.

'But you don't . . .'

Rumbold anticipated her question. 'I'm a trained saboteur.'

'Why didn't you tell Crispian?'

'You never gave me the opportunity, Joanna. Before I had a chance to volunteer, you'd already told him that you were an expert in helicopter engines. I merely came to see a real expert at work!' His voice was mocking, but there was no malice in his eyes. 'No more questions. Keep watch and alert me if any more death squad commandos arrive. I won't be long.'

'How can I alert you without waking the castle?'

'Use your speciality.'

'What's that?'

'Improvise!'

Joanna crouched near a gunship and kept watch. She saw the sunrise, a pale glow that stretched along the length of the horizon like light leaking from beneath a badly fitted door. She grew impatient but resisted the temptation to call out to Rumbold. 'Where is he?' Joanna thought. 'If we don't leave soon, we'll be caught.'

She listened attentively but could hear nothing. A hand touched her lightly on the shoulder. She swung round and found Rumbold leaning over her.

'It's done. The gunships will never fly again,' he whispered. 'Run for the kitchen door. I've one last job to do.' He pushed Joanna towards the door. 'Run! Don't look back!'

Joanna raced across the courtyard, but before she reached the door there was a violent explosion. A tornado of heat and suffocating smoke tore into her back, scorching her hair and neck. She staggered through the door and then halted in alarm. The kitchen staff were already at work. The sound of the explosion and the sudden appearance of Joanna paralysed them. Joanna stood silhouetted in the doorway, a wild figure daubed in forbidden colours, with smoke and flames leaping about her.

'It's the devil!' cried the chief cook, and his eyes bulged from his head with fear.

'If it be not the devil himself,' shouted an apprentice cook, 'it be one of his most horrible demons. I've never seen such an ugly fiend!'

Joanna was not flattered by his comment, but she used it to her advantage. She let out a terrible shriek, twisted her face into a mask of cruelty and leaped upon the table, her hands striking out at the cooks like claws.

'God forgive me,' pleaded the young apprentice. 'I'll never cheat at cards again, never steal another side of bacon or a bottle of wine. Never!' He was just about to continue his confession when Rumbold burst through the door, his kilt in tatters and his upper body streaked and burned. 'O mercy! Mercy!' gabbled the boy. 'It's the devil himself, and he's hardly wearing a stitch.' He crossed himself religiously, and there was such an expression of horror on his face that Joanna was tempted to laugh. Instead, she responded to his plea for mercy by delivering a sharp kick to his jaw which sent him tumbling to the floor.

The apprentice had been so positioned that he had concealed Joanna's karate kick from the rest of the kitchen staff. They had merely seen her capering on the table, and then the youth suddenly collapsed and lay twitching on the floor. 'She has the power,' screamed a cook. 'She's killed the boy with the evil eye.'

Rumbold grasped the situation immediately and added some special effects of his own. 'Flee for your lives, human trash, before it's too late. We've come to feast in your kitchen,' he snarled in an evil, unearthly voice. 'Speak a word of our feasting and we'll bear you hence to our lair of brimstone and torment.' The cooks rushed for the door and fled from the kitchen in terror.

Rumbold winked at Joanna and then pointed at the unconscious apprentice. 'You've been improvising again, I see. The poor boy will have nightmares for the rest of his life. You've probably spoiled a promising career in catering.' A babble of voices interrupted him. 'Run, Joanna. Follow as near to me as you can. The burning gunships will act as a decoy, but we might be unlucky and run into a death squad or a patrol of secret police. Run!'

A series of dull explosions shook the interior of the castle, dislodging a meteorite shower of masonry on Joanna and Rumbold.

'What's that?' asked Joanna, looking anxiously about her.

'I have no idea, and I'm certainly not going to investigate. Run!'

Joanna sped after Rumbold. He adjusted his pace to suit hers and kept about a metre ahead, using the vast girth of his body to shield her in the event of a surprise attack. They raced along the final length of corridor, swept round the corner, and there before them was the door of Crispian's apartment. Guns exploded with sharp *crack, cracks* and bullets whistled around them, ricocheting from the walls. A death squad patrol occupied the short stairway that led to the door, and their guns were jolting and smoking in their hands as they fired on the giant and his companion.

Rumbold staggered as a bullet ripped into his lower arm; another dug a deep furrow in his cheek. He was about to retreat when the apartment door burst open and the nazdarg hurled himself at the attackers, the blades of his hands felling the commandos like saplings before the axe. As they turned to face the new menace, the giant leaped among them, his legs and arms moving in a whir of speed, scything through

85

the death squad and cutting them from the stairway. Joanna followed hard on his heels, marvelling at his agility and strength.

She saw the commando rise—his skin stretched taut against his skull, hair short-cropped and eyes like festering cuts. She saw his two-fisted grip on the gun, saw him level it at Rumbold's chest, saw his finger tighten on the trigger, saw a grin of savage triumph twist his lips, and then she sprang, throwing her body between the commando and the giant. The gun detonated with a crash, kicking upwards in a spurt of flame, and red hot pain surged through her body. As she pitched forward, she felt arms encircle her and a raw, anguished voice sounded in her ears: 'Why did you do that, Joanna?'

Coldness spread across her body and numbed the agony. She smiled weakly at Rumbold and tried to focus on his face, but it was shrouded in mist. 'I was just improvising,' she whispered, and then a roaring darkness swept over her and carried her away.

15

The Journey

Joanna struggled to open her eyes, but her lids seemed glued together by a powerful adhesive. A low throbbing filled her senses. Her body throbbed, a raw pulse of pain that spread outward in tiny temors from the flesh below her left shoulder. But there was also another sound: a harsh, insistent rhythm that beat time with the throbbing in her shoulder. Thoughts came slowly like feet trudging through sludge. The throbbing sound was familiar. Yes, there was something she must remember. She knew that it was there, lurking like a trout in a shaded pool. She reached for it, but it slithered through her fingers and sped away. She slipped back into darkness, and when she returned, everything was clearer. She remembered the sharp crack of the gun, the flash of fire, the world toppling about her and the angry shouts of men. She struggled to sit up and felt hands restraining her. 'Lay still, Joanna, or the wound will open.' She sighed and opened her eyes. Dark clouds fluttered above her like a flock of squawking crows, and the sun oozed light into a lead-grey sky.

'Where are we? What's happening?'

'Be still and rest,' said the voice, 'and thanks for saving me.' The voice was gentle and sincere.

Joanna turned and found Rumbold with her eyes; the movement drove needles of pain into her shoulder and chest. 'If I'd known it was going to hurt this much,' she groaned, 'I'd never have done it.' She groaned again and sat up. Rumbold was seated on the boot of the Jaguar, and his legs straddled the rear of the car and disappeared over the front passenger seat. The wound on his cheek had been roughly stitched and his right arm was in a sling.

Stephen glanced over his shoulder at Joanna. 'How's the patient?'

'Terrible!'

'You'll live. The bullet left a neat hole under your shoulder. Martha dressed the wound as best she could and put a poultice on it, but it will hurt badly for a week or two.'

The sleek Jaguar sped across the flatlands, its engine throbbing loudly in the silence. They came to a deserted town and raced through it, the roar of their progress echoing eerily in empty streets and buildings. Joanna tried again. 'What's happening? Where are we?'

'We're escaping,' replied Rumbold. 'Now try to rest.'

'Not before you tell me what's happening.'

'You're stubborn, Joanna. If you want to recover quickly, you must rest.'

'How do you expect me to rest, man, with a bullet hole in my shoulder?' she said, lapsing into her mother's Jamaican accent. The pain made her short-tempered. 'Get on with it, man. Tell me why I'm here.'

'After you were shot, I carried you into Crispian and Martha's apartment. Martha's a doctor by profession. She sterilised your wound, bandaged it and gave you a shot of morphine to deaden the pain. The explosions that we heard were the work of Stephen. He sabotaged the communications centre. The president wanted a high security fortress in the middle of nowhere. He never anticipated that it would become his temporary prison. His gunships are destroyed, he can't make contact with the outside world and his prisoners have escaped with a senior nazdarg sergeant. You can be sure he's not having a good day.

'The burning gunships gave us the decoy that we needed. While attention was diverted and the police and death squads searched the castle for us, Crispian took us down a secret stairway to his garage.'

'His garage?'

'It's more like an underground bunker. The stair-case ends at the entrance of a passageway that leads to the bunker. It's situated about five or six hundred metres north-east of the castle's walls, but still within range of hostile fire. We were fortunate. The president's forces were divided between those who were trying to salvage the gunships and communication equipment, and the "hunt and kill" patrols who were searching for us. Our departure took them completely by surprise. They fired off a few rounds but they were way off target.'

'What happened to Crispian and Martha?'

'They're following us. It would be suicide for them to remain in the castle. They're already linked with our escape. They're chugging along behind in a vintage Bentley. It's a marvellous old car, but no match for this sleek cat.'

'Where are we heading?'

'We're going to try to locate an outlaw band. They may be able to give us information on the where-abouts of Adriana. Stephen thinks he can track them down.'

The car sped eastward, and behind it the grey sun slipped over the edge of the world and night crept upon the land. A spasm of pain made Joanna cry out. 'This is worse than toothache,' she whispered bravely, but her eyes shone with tears. Her body felt heavy and unreal, but her mind was as light as a floating dandelion seed. 'I think I'll sleep,' she thought, and then she remembered that there was a question that she wanted to ask Rumbold. 'Why did you blow up the gunships?'

'To divert attention from our escape and destroy the fuel dump,' he replied, but before he had time to explain his action further, Joanna had slumped across the seat and was asleep.

She awoke to the gentle sound of snores. Stephen lay slumped across the steering wheel, his head pillowed in his arms, and Rumbold lay asleep on a pile of hay. The sun was already brightening the east, and the air was clean and bracing. Joanna breathed deeply, but the sudden splaying of her ribs stoked her wound and sent sparks of pain through her body. 'Ouch!' She sat up very carefully, nursing her injured shoulder. The front passenger door was open, so she climbed over the seat in front of her and lowered herself gently onto the ground. Rumbold stirred and sat up.

'Do you need any help?' he whispered, aware that Stephen was asleep.

'No, I'm okay. My shoulder's hurting me, but I need to stretch my legs.'

'Do you mind if I come with you?'

'You're welcome! Where are we?'

'About five hundred metres from the sea. The outlaw bands are supposed to inhabit this area. Stephen thinks they'll make contact with us. They're constantly being joined by new recruits.'

'Who are they?'

'Most of the recruits are people who're unhappy with the president and his government. The outlaw bands survive by vigilance. Stephen thinks that we've already been identified and reckons they'll make contact with us today, so keep alert.'

'Look!' said Joanna, her eyes bright with excitement.

Rumbold followed the direction of her gaze. An airship sailed over the edge of the horizon, towing in its wake the golden sun. The east was ablaze with light, a great tide of flame that swept into the sky and rolled towards them. 'Deliverance has come!' shouted Rumbold, and he began to leap and dance with joy, forgetful of the pain in his arm.

But as he shouted, a vast breaker of grey smog crashed over them and roared out to meet the light. For a few moments, golden dawn held the grey smog at bay, but not for long. The wall of flame faltered and was breached in many places, and then it fell and the grey tidal wave burst over it, drowning the light. But still the airship came on, and lightning writhed about it. Beneath the airship, the sky and sea turned blue and the grey was tossed aside.

'The Captain's coming! The Captain's coming!' cried Joanna. 'That's his airship.'

A shout startled them: 'Help me! He . . .!' The voice trailed into silence. It was Stephen's voice.

16

The Outlaws

Rumbold burst through the ring of outlaws and lifted Stephen from the ground, nursing him in his arms like a child. He was unconscious, and his body and head were lacerated with tiny cuts from the beating. An outlaw aimed a blow at Rumbold with his staff, but the giant stopped the blow with his foot and broke the staff.

'Beware, little man,' he warned. 'I could break you as I have broken your stick. Is this how you greet friends?'

The leader of the outlaws stepped forward. 'He's no friend,' he snarled, 'but one of Dimrat's buddies. It was he who led the patrol that hunted Adriana. I'll never forget his stinking face. Nazdarg scum! When he and his filthy chums couldn't find her, they tortured the outlaws who sheltered her just for the fun of it.'

Joanna stumbled into the circle of angry men and took her place beside Rumbold. 'He is a friend,' she said, but her voice was faint and blood welled from the wound beneath her shoulder. 'He saved us from the president and Dimrat. Without him, we would probably be dead. His name is Stephen, and he is now the servant of the Captain.'

The outlaws looked at Joanna in astonishment. 'You look as if you need a doctor, kid,' said the leader, 'or else you'll be as grey as us soon.' Anger fled his eyes, to be replaced by concern and wonder.

'Sit down, kid, and let me try to do something with that wound. It's the first time I've ever seen red blood.'

'It will be the last time, boss, if you don't act quickly. The kid's haemorrhaging. Let me have a go.

I used to drive an ambulance. I still remember some of the first aid stuff I was taught.' A short, balding man stepped forward and examined Joanna's wound. 'This is bad news, boss. She needs a doc quick, or she'll bleed to death otherwise.'

The leader looked up at Rumbold. 'We've already heard about this kid. She and another guy caused mayhem in the capital. For several days now, large numbers of recruits have been joining our bands. They all tell the same story: two illegals, an old guy with a guitar and a tall girl with funny clothes, held a concert outside the government buildings. The girl was captured by the president's boys and taken away in a gunship, but the old man vanished into thin air. He must be some guy. They're still singing his songs.'

'Boss, leave your explanations for later. We need to get this kid back to camp or she's a goner. What are you going to do about the nazdarg?'

'Bring him along.' He turned to Rumbold and looked at him suspiciously. 'You're responsible for him. If we have any trouble, you're both dead meat.'

Rumbold smiled at the outlaw leader engagingly. 'I have no intention of being butchered,' he said, and then he nodded in the direction of the sea. 'We have company!'

The outlaws swung round and cried out in alarm: 'It's an airship. It must be one of Dimrat's inventions. Run for cover!'

Joanna's mind had a frosty clarity, but she was very weak. The pain in her shoulder had given way to a numbing cold. While the outlaws had been discussing her condition, she had fixed her eyes on the airship and watched its progress across the sky. The throb of its engine had ceased, and it moved silently towards the company, turning sea and land beneath it to their original colours. 'Don't run,' she pleaded, and her voice was little more than a whisper. 'It's the Captain. Would Dimrat restore colour to the land?'

'The kid's talking sense. I've heard of this Captain fellow and . . .'

But before the leader could finish the sentence, the airship floated into the airspace above them and stopped. One moment, the outlaws were grey figures in a grey landscape, and the next, they were daubed with colour. Their astonishment was so great that they lost their fear of the airship, but as they marvelled at the colours it grew steadily closer, filling the sky above them like a new world. A hatch opened, a rope ladder swung towards them and two figures swiftly descended.

'Is that dark bloke the Captain?' asked the outlaw leader.

'Yes,' mumbled Joanna.

'And who's that tall woman with the weird clothes?'

'I think her name's Valsa, but I'm not sure.'

The Captain and Valsa sprang from the ladder. The Captain greeted the outlaws with a salute and smile, beckoned to Valsa to follow and knelt beside Joanna.

'Hello,' he whispered, and his fingers probed the wound in her shoulder. 'You'll be all right in a day or two. I've brought Valsa to care for you. She's a gifted healer.'

Joanna smiled. 'The pain's gone, but I feel very cold. I haven't been able to bring the colour back to the land. You must be disappointed in me.'

'On the contrary, Joanna. Without you knowing it, you've already started a revolution in this country. Do not be afraid. You will triumph over the grey and see this land adorned in colour.' The Captain turned to Valsa. 'I put Joanna in your charge. Care for her well.'

The Captain left Joanna and took Stephen from the arms of Rumbold. His eyes were gentle, and his voice flowed into the nazdarg's heart like a healing cordial. 'Wake up, my son. There is no need to be afraid.'

Rumbold attempted to interfere. 'He's badly injured, sir. The outlaws beat him senseless.'

'These tiny scratches are nothing. His deepest wound cannot be seen. He is a man, Rumbold, in the body of a nazdarg. He fears that people will see the nazdarg and reject the man within. He could easily have defended himself against the outlaws but did not wish to hurt them. He has already inflicted terrible suffering on the outlaw bands and could not bear to hurt them again.'

The Captain took the nazdarg's head in both his hands and whispered in his ear: 'Wake up, my son. There is no need to be afraid. The outlaws will embrace you as a brother, and you will be a father to the orphans of the land.'

Stephen opened his eyes and gazed in wonder at the Captain. 'Is this a dream or are you real?'

'I'm real, my son, and I'll be staying with you for a day or two.'

Stephen laughed, and his eyes gleamed like sapphires. 'There's no need to carry me. I'll walk. I always feel safe when you're near.'

Joanna was lifted into the back of the Jaguar, her head resting on Valsa's lap. Valsa removed the poultice from the wound and touched it lightly with her fingertips. A soft pulse of energy flowed into the wound and rippled across her body. The tingling sensation was rather like pins and needles, but much more pleasant. Joanna shivered with pleasure. 'How did you do that?'

'Be still,' said Valsa gently, 'and I'll explain later.'

The agony returned to Joanna's shoulder, and she bit her lip, stifling a scream. 'The pain's terrible. Can't you do anything about it?' Valsa didn't reply, but the pressure of her fingertips increased and waves of energy flooded into the wound. The pain subsided and then vanished altogether. Peace! The gnawing pain had disappeared and Joanna felt as if she hung suspended in warm, clear water. The blood stopped trickling from the wound, and the angry swelling on her shoulder grew fainter: a shadow on her olive skin like bruising on an apple.

'I feel sleepy,' she whispered, and she smothered a yawn with her hand. She searched for Valsa with her eyes, but the world about her was losing its sharpness and clarity; she tried to thank Valsa for her kindness, but her words were jumbled like notes struck at random on a piano. 'Sorry! Can't stay awake,' she mumbled and she fell into a warm, buoyant sea of sleep.

Rumbold accompanied the outlaw leader to the car. The outlaw leaped over the driver's door without bothering to open it and adjusted the seat to his leg length. 'Your nazdarg mate's gone with the Captain. Jump in and ride with us.'

'Thanks for the offer,' he said, 'but I'll run behind. If you keep the speed to about thirty, I'll be able to keep up.'

'You must be joking, mate. Thirty miles an hour in this baby! I've been dreaming of driving one of these for years. You either sit in the back or march home with the rest of my boys. It's only seven miles to our camp.'

'I'll march. My legs are cramped from sitting and I desperately need exercise,' said Rumbold, 'but just make sure you remember that one of your passengers is seriously injured.'

'Is she okay?' he asked, addressing the question at Valsa.

Valsa nodded and smiled up at the giant. 'Don't worry. In a couple of days she'll be better.'

'A couple of days?' said Rumbold in amazement. 'That's a bullet hole, not a wasp sting.' But before he could protest further, he was interrupted by the outlaw leader.

'Don't worry, lady,' he said, turning to Valsa with an expression of mock sympathy on his face, 'we can outrun the big guy and give you and your patient some peace. This baby can hit a ton before his legs start moving. We'll be out of earshot before he has time to open his mouth again.' The engine purred and then howled as the outlaw's foot hit the accelerator pedal, but nothing happened. Rumbold had lifted the rear of the car and the wheels were spinning helplessly in the air.

'Rear wheel drive,' said Rumbold, and he grinned crookedly at the driver. 'A bit primitive, but I wouldn't like to spoil your pleasure!' He leaped to one side and the tyres bit the tarmac, skidded and left snakes of blistering rubber on the road. The Jaguar hurtled forward, the outlaw's yell of triumph lost in the engine roar and the gap that quickly opened between the giant and the car. Rumbold sprang after it, running with long, graceful strides, his feet beating a gentle tattoo on the surface of the road.

After he had run several miles, he felt a light touch on his thigh. He turned and saw two young men in strange suits with large shoulder pads racing at his heels. Their feet skimmed the road and they kept pace with him effortlessly. 'Are you Rumbold?' said the shortest of the duo.

'Yes!'

'The Captain said you'll need help to find the outlaws' camp. We're going to carry you all the way. Stop!'

Rumbold jerked to a halt. 'Carry me, boys? You'll need a big pram!'

Rumbold's laughter turned to utter astonishment. The boys clamped their arms about his legs. 'Okay, Edwin. We'll instruct our audio beacons on a count of three. Ready! One, two, three. Altitude: two thousand metres. Speed: twenty mezilons.' The earth tore away from Rumbold, and the wind screamed in his ears.

'Let me down, boys,' he shouted. 'I don't have a head for heights.'

Thor and Edwin laughed. 'It's too late, sir,' replied Edwin. 'Just close your eyes and imagine what that outlaw will say when he finds you've beaten him to the camp.'

'And don't struggle,' added Thor. 'We wouldn't like to drop you.'

Rumbold went limp but his hands were clenched in tight fists and his knuckles shone. 'Make this a quick flight, boys,' he pleaded.

Thor pretended to misunderstand. 'You want something sensational? Acrobatics? A low flight obstacle course? A vertical nose dive? Free fall?'

'Keep it simple, boys. Nothing elaborate! Just get me to the camp as quickly as possible. This is not my idea of pleasure.'

They were flying at such high altitude that Rumbold lost his feeling of vertigo. 'I could learn to enjoy this,' he said cautiously. 'It's like windsurfing in a tornado.'

The land tipped towards them and they began the descent. 'We've arrived,' said Edwin. The ocean sparkled below, and Rumbold could see the grey surf breaking on the beach.

'Where's the camp?' he enquired. 'I can't see any sign of it.'

'There!' said Edwin, and he pointed in the direction of a canyon that rose vertically from the sea and swept inland in magical formations of rock. 'The canyon is honeycombed with caves and tunnels. It's the ideal haven, safe from nazdargs and death squad commandos.' Edwin nodded at Thor. 'Ready?'

'Yeah!'

'Hold on tight, Rumbold.'

'What do you intend to do?' he asked, his eyes flitting nervously from one brother to the other.

'Drop in for tea,' said Thor. 'One, two, three! Power dive to ground level.'

The somersault seemed to drive Rumbold's stomach

into his mouth. Earth and sky swivelled and changed positions. For a fragment of a second he hung in the sky, and then he was falling, a missile aimed at the heart of the earth. The canyon leaped to meet him, a jumble of fantastic shapes: alien worlds swarming with monsters; fantasies erupting from stone. Rumbold was a giant with superhuman powers, but compared with such glory he was nothing.

In seconds, the rocks of the canyon were so near that he turned his head away and threw out his arms to protect himself, bracing his body for the impact— but it never came. 'Horizontal mode and lock into location sequence,' commanded the brothers.

The vertical drop turned into a steep curve and flattened out, and Rumbold was hurtling across the canyon, hugging its contours. A sheer wall of rock loomed ahead, yet still he sped on. At the last moment he swerved upwards in a vertical climb, the boys yelling with excitement on either side of him, straightened out and dropped into the dark mouth of a cave. The boys' yells were repeated by the echoes, and then they were flying blind into the guts of the canyon.

17

The Camp

They flew into the cave like blind bats, the faint glimmer from the cave entrance quickly extinguished by darkness. Each movement came without warning. One moment they were hurtling forward as straight as a laser, and in the next they were swerving sharply to the right or left. Thor and Edwin greeted each wild twist and turn with a medley of yells. 'Hey, man,' shouted Edwin, 'this is better than the light speed simulator at the Cosmo Fair. Wow!'

Rumbold didn't share the brothers' enthusiasm. The darkness and speed of the journey confused him, so he counted out loud, his voice cloned by echoes until it seemed as if he had shattered into many selves.

'One, two, three, four, five, six—a sharp swerve to the left and a terrifying drop into darkness.

Thor screamed with excitement: 'Wow, that was a real "neuro-blaster".'

'Seven, eight, nine, ten, eleven, twelve, thirteen'— flying in a straight line. In the distance, the drip, drip of falling water. 'Fourteen, fifteen'—a sudden drop, followed by a steep turn to the left. 'Sixteen, seventeen, eighteen'—jumping unseen obstacles.

Thor and Edwin were yelling at the tops of their voices. 'This is wild, man,' gasped Thor breathlessly. 'It's the nearest I've ever come to riding a rodeo. Do you want to go back and do it again?'

Edwin was about to answer when Rumbold inter-rupted. 'Just keep going straight on, boys. There'll be thrills enough ahead.' And then he resumed his counting: 'Nineteen, twenty, twenty-one, twenty-two, twenty-three, twenty-four, twenty-five'—the roar of water and spray on his face. 'Twenty-six, twenty-seven, twenty-eight, twenty-nine, thirty, thirty-one, thirty . . .' But before he completed the number, the flight came to an abrupt halt. Rumbold regained his calm as soon as his feet touched the ground. 'What's wrong?' he enquired.

'Nothing, as far as we know,' said Thor cautiously. 'We've given our audio beacons the correct co-ordinates, so we must have arrived.'

Rumbold probed the wall with his fingers. 'We've arrived. There's a door in this wall, but no latch or handle. I hope there's someone on the other side.' He beat against it with his fists and shouted: 'Please open the door. We're friends.' But there was no response. 'Okay, I'll have to open it from this side!'

'And how do you intend to do that?' asked Thor, expecting a high tech explanation.

'I'll kick it down!'

Rumbold's first kick splintered the door, and his second tore it from its hinges and sent it crashing to the floor. A dim light dripped through the entrance, but it was too weak to make any real impact on the darkness. Rumbold and the brothers leaped across the broken door into a short length of unlit passageway that joined a wide corridor. Electric light bulbs spanned its length, hanging from the ceiling like a string of luminous pearls.

'There's colour here,' said Rumbold. 'Either the Captain's nearby, or this place is the last fortress of colour in the land.'

'When we last visited this canyon fortress,' said Edwin, 'it was as grey as any other part of the land. The Captain's arrived.'

Further conversation was silenced by the beat of running feet. A band of armed outlaws raced towards them. The leader of the patrol caught sight of Rumbold and his face softened. He smiled with pleasure. 'It's okay, they're friends,' he said, and he ran towards Rumbold. 'I thought I'd never see you again, Rumbold. I was told that you were caged in the president's fortress. The Captain brought me the good news of your rescue and escape. You're a hard man to kill.'

'Benedict! Benedict!' laughed the giant joyfully. 'You always arrive when I need you most. It's a pity that you weren't here a minute or two earlier, or you'd have saved your door.'

Rumbold picked the man up like a child and they embraced. 'I think that you're still growing, old friend,' said Benedict as the giant placed him gently on his feet.

'I wish I could say the same for you,' laughed Rumbold as he looked down at the small figure that stood before him.

The giant turned to Thor and Edwin. 'Don't be deceived by his size. This man is the greatest warrior in the land. He's done more damage to the cause of Dimrat than a whole army.' The brothers greeted Benedict politely. He was short and lean with dark, intelligent eyes, and he buzzed with such energy that he seemed to be moving even when he was standing still.

Benedict studied the boys for a few moments and then smiled, his face overflowing with warmth. 'Welcome, Thor and Edwin. The Captain's warned us about your arrival.' He turned to Rumbold and a humorous gleam danced in his eyes. 'I hope you enjoyed the flight.'

'It was unforgettable,' said Rumbold, rolling each vowel, 'almost as "unforgettable" as our little flight in the hijacked gunship.'

'Oh, so you still remember that!' said Benedict, raising his eyebrows in mock surprise. 'An interesting experience.'

'Interesting? Why didn't you tell me that you'd never flown a gunship before?'

'I thought it was unimportant. We're still alive so why complain?' Before the giant could reply, Benedict turned to the patrol and his voice crackled with authority. 'Replace the door immediately and set a twenty-four-hour guard on it.' He signalled to a slender, blonde-haired woman. 'You take responsibility for the rota, Sergeant Denise, and report back to me.'

'Yes sir!' she said and gave a crisp salute.

*   *   *

The Captain and Stephen stood side by side and gazed at the land below from a ballroom window.

'That's our destination,' said the Captain, and he pointed to the canyon. 'The outlaw bands have used its caverns and tunnels as hideaways for years, but recently they've become more organised.'

'Why is that?' asked Stephen inquisitively.

'A new leader has emerged called Benedict.'

'Benedict!' exclaimed Stephen in amazement. 'The guerrilla leader?'

'Yes!'

Stephen laughed. 'Dimrat's in big trouble. Benedict was the most brilliant and daring of all the guerrilla leaders, a name that struck fear into the hearts of the nazdargs and death squad commandos alike. We were informed that he had fled from the land. The president believed him to be the most dangerous enemy of his government. Rumbold was a loner, but Benedict was a capable organiser and a fantastic leader of men and women. His followers were fanatics. How did he team up with the outlaws?'

'I suggested it to him,' said the Captain. 'He's organised the outlaws into a very capable fighting force.'

'I can believe it,' said Stephen, and he gave a low whistle of astonishment.

The airship floated across the canyon, and the grey rock flamed yellow and red. Tiny figures ran from the opening of a large cavern and stood in little groups, waving in welcome.

'It's time to meet the outlaws,' said the Captain, and he guided the nazdarg towards the exit.

'I can't go. I can't!' said Stephen, his eyes troubled like pools of blue water lashed by a violent wind.

'They won't want me. They'll always remember that I'm a nazdarg and a killer of outlaws.'

The Captain turned and smiled at him tenderly. 'You are my son, Stephen, and anyone who rejects you rejects me. Don't be afraid. Friends and great joy await you.'

The Captain and Stephen sprang from the last rung of the rope ladder and greeted the people.

'Why did you bring a nazdarg here?' asked a tall man who walked with a limp. 'It was a nazdarg who crippled me.'

A chorus of hostile voices rose in agreement:

'We don't want any nazdarg scum here.'

'Get him away.'

'Shoot him!'

'Throw him from a cliff top.'

Stephen cowered behind the Captain, his hands making tiny movements as if he was trying to ward off their hatred. The Captain raised his hand and silenced the people. 'This is my son,' he said, 'and his name is Stephen.'

'How can he be, mate? He's a filthy nazdarg.'

The Captain's eyes flared with light. 'Have you ever known me to lie to you or deceive you, Reg?'

The man looked uncomfortable. 'No, but how can you have a son who's a nazdarg? It's impossible.'

'I've adopted him. He shares my name, and any insult offered to him is an insult to me. Apart from his nazdarg shape, he is no different from any of you. He's rebelled against Dimrat and is a true outlaw, but I'll let him speak for himself.' The Captain stepped back and placed his hand supportively on Stephen's shoulder. 'Speak,' he whispered, 'and their hearts will open.'

Stephen told his story, and as he spoke the hostility left their eyes. He hid nothing from them. The outlaws were an appreciative audience and cheered him loudly when he told them of the rescue of Rumbold and Joanna.

'Next time you have a punch-up with the secret police, sonny,' shouted a tubby woman who was nursing a baby, 'give them one for me.'

'And me,' said a lady with a sad, haunted face and greying hair. 'They took my husband and children away to a labour camp. I haven't seen them for fifteen years.'

Stephen looked at the woman kindly. 'I wish I could help you, but I'm certain of one thing.'

'What is that?' she asked, and hope kindled in her eyes.

'That Dimrat's power will soon be broken and we shall be free again.'

A great cheer and clapping greeted his statement.

A girl of about five years of age ran from the circle of onlookers and stood in front of Stephen. Her hair was untidy and one knee was lightly grazed. 'Hello,' Stephen said, and he knelt down to talk to her. 'What is your name?' The girl wriggled nervously and stood on one leg. 'Don't be afraid,' he coaxed, and his blue eyes shone with gentleness.

'Marianne,' she said shyly, and all of a sudden Stephen was surrounded by laughing, curious children.

'Do you really eat human beings for dinner?' asked a skinny, black boy.

Stephen smiled and pretended to look fierce. 'Only if they don't behave themselves and obey their parents.'

'You won't eat me, then,' he said, looking relieved, 'because I don't have a dad and mum.'

'Nor do I,' said Marianne, and she slipped her hand into Stephen's and smiled up at him. He returned the smile, surprised at how easily he could talk to children.

'If you don't mind,' said the Captain, 'I'll leave you with your new friends. I've some important business to attend to. Rumbold and Joanna are already here, and Crispian and Martha will arrive soon. Outlaw patrols are already searching for them. I'll see you in an hour or two.' He smiled and touched the nazdarg lightly on the shoulder. 'You gave a fine speech, Stephen. You're quite a public speaker.'

The children seized Stephen's hands and led him into the cavern, their voices twittering like a flock of excited birds. The Captain paused and watched him for a few moments: a huge, rambling figure swamped in boys and girls.

'You've found a home, my son,' he whispered, and he strode away to hold counsel with Benedict and Rumbold.

In the north and west, clouds were gathering as Dimrat prepared his legions.

18

The Attack

The gunships swarmed across the horizon, turning the skyline dark.

Five days had passed since Joanna had come to the canyon, and in that time Valsa had performed miracles. Her wound had healed, leaving only a faint scar, and she had recovered her strength. Crispian and Martha had arrived safely and were given a tumultuous welcome by the outlaws, and the Captain's airship floated like a banner above the canyon fortress. And then, at dawn on the sixth day, the gunships appeared. As the first rays of sunlight burst like shrapnel over the eastern ridge of the canyon, the attack began. Joanna awoke to the shriek of a siren and the heavy thud of explosions. The canyon echoed with the sound of running feet and the urgent babble of voices. She quickly pulled on her clothes, tied the laces of her trainers and threw open the heavy door of her apartment. A group of well-armed outlaws dashed towards her.

'What's going on?' she asked.

'We're being attacked,' said the leader of the group and sped on.

'I'll try to find Rumbold and Stephen and see if I can help,' she thought, and she raced to the room they shared. The door was ajar, but there was no sign of either of them. She ran towards the main entrance of the cavern, but was stopped by an outlaw officer.

'You can't go any further, Miss,' he warned. 'Only military personnel are allowed beyond this point.'

'I was looking for Rumbold and Stephen. Have you seen them?'

'You mean the nazdarg and the giant? Yes, I've seen them, Miss. They're with the patrol that's defending the front entrance. All children and non-combatants are to be evacuated to the deeper levels of the canyon. You must join them.'

'Can't I help? I could run messages.'

'Orders are orders. Miss, so please leave this sector immediately.'

Joanna was about to protest when a huge explosion shook the canyon, the blast roaring along the tunnel towards her like an express train. Joanna turned and ran, but the blast caught her and threw her from her feet, the dust and debris stinging her skin and choking her. She lay on the floor for several seconds, and then climbed shakily to her feet, her body wracked by coughs. The dust was suffocating. It made her eyes smart, itched at the back of her throat and clogged her nostrils like a foul smelling mucus.

The officer lay on his back, and his breath came in painful gasps. His temple was swollen, and a bruise spread across his face like spilled ink. Joanna tore off her pullover and placed it beneath the officer's head as a pillow. He groaned, and his breathing became more regular.

'Ill get help,' she whispered, and she squeezed the officer's hand reassuringly. 'You'll be okay. You'll

106

just have a bad headache for a few hours.' The officer's revolver bulged from a holster at his thigh. 'I'd better take this,' she said, 'just in case I meet any of Dimrat's soldiers. I don't think you'll be needing it.'

As she crouched over the officer, a nazdarg leaped through the dust cloud and sprang towards her. Joanna gripped the gun in both hands, pointed it at the creature and pulled the trigger, but nothing happened.

'Put that gun down, Joanna,' commanded a familiar voice. It was Stephen.

Joanna trembled. 'I could have killed you. I pulled the trigger but nothing happened.'

'Thank goodness! I'm just beginning to enjoy being alive. Before you can fire that revolver, you must lift the safety catch.' He took the revolver and showed Joanna how to do it. 'There! It's simple. But make sure you don't blow away your friends.' He gave Joanna a quick smile. 'I'd hate you to be lonely!' Stephen picked up the officer. 'We've no time to hang around. Dimrat's legions have broken through our first line of defence. One of their missiles destroyed the opening to the cavern. That was the big explosion.'

As he spoke, Rumbold and a company of outlaws joined them. 'Benedict is involved in a rear guard action,' said the giant. 'He and his troops are holding back the enemy, but they'll fall back soon. The trap seems to be working.'

'What trap?' demanded Joanna.

'I can't tell you now. And anyway, who gave you permission to be in the war zone? You're supposed to be recovering from a bullet wound.'

Joanna was about to reply when the *tat-a-tat* of gunfire broke out nearby. Benedict and his troops retreated towards them, hugging the walls of the tunnel to make themselves less of a target for enemy fire. One soldier sprang into the centre of the tunnel and began to shoot out the lightbulbs, but before she could finish her task a sniper shot her down. Benedict crawled over to the soldier and hauled her to safety.

'We'll get you out of here, Angelique,' he said and caressed her cheek with his hand. She tried to speak, but a trickle of blood bubbled from the corner of her mouth.

The retreat was not a rout but a well-disciplined manoeuvre. Benedict held his small force together, luring the enemy deeper into the canyon. 'Dimrat thinks he's fighting small, poorly organised gangs of outlaws,' whispered Stephen to Joanna. 'He'd think twice about coming in here if he knew that Benedict was around.' The nazdarg chuckled, and his blue eyes shone fiercely.

The tunnel opened into a wide chamber, and lurking behind rocks and hidden in passageways were Benedict's forces. Joanna saw Crispian, his rifle aimed at the tunnel entrance and a two-handed machete hanging from his waist. Rumbold propelled Joanna into a passage. 'Stay there,' he commanded, 'and keep your head down. And no heroics.'

Benedict and the remains of his company slid into the cavern carrying their injured companions. Valsa appeared and, assisted by a group of the older outlaws, carried the wounded away.

Joanna hid in the mouth of the passage and waited, her revolver ready in her hand. A terrible howl shook the cavern and splintered into a thousand echoes; a gigantic nazdarg leaped from the tunnel and stood peering into the gloom, the hair on his spine bristling and upright. The outlaws waited for Benedict's signal. Benedict was crouching next to Rumbold. He leaned over to the giant and whispered in his ear: 'He's yours, but do it quickly.' Rumbold slipped from his side like a shadow and sped soundlessly towards the nazdarg, his body bent double and hidden by a circle of boulders that had been arranged around the chamber as a defensive wall. The nazdarg was still peering uncertainly into the gloom when Rumbold sprang at him. His mouth opened in a howl, but no sound breached his lips. A fist pounded into the side of his skull and his world shattered like the starburst of an exploding shell. His legs sagged and he tumbled into the waiting arms of Rumbold. The giant dragged him behind a boulder and returned to his position.

'Dead?' enquired Benedict.

'Asleep!' said the giant.

Benedict looked at him curiously. 'A year ago he'd have been dead.'

'That was a year ago,' said the giant, and he gave him a lopsided smile.

Stephen appeared and squeezed the giant's shoulder. 'Thanks for sparing the nazdarg. He was one of the first batch and I think he came looking for me. If he was leading the vanguard, there'd have been others following him.'

'Why did he come looking for you?' asked Rumbold.

'For the same reason that I rescued you and Joanna. It must be the Captain's work.'

Benedict gave a low, humourless laugh. 'We shoot them and the Captain wins their hearts!'

A sound startled them. The nazdarg staggered to his feet and leaned against the boulder. His voice was hoarse and words were forced from his lips with a tremendous effort of will: 'Run! Run! The kilvarsts are here. Run! You're betrayed.' He slid slowly to the floor, his hands clawing at the smooth rock of the boulder for leverage. 'If you escape, tell nazdarg number 362d that . . .' But his strength failed before he could complete the message, and he slumped forward and was still.

Stephen was about to run to the assistance of the nazdarg, when Benedict restrained him. 'Who's nazdarg number 362d?'

'Me!'

'And the kilvarsts?'

'Only rumours, but word reached us that Dimrat was going to replace the nazdarg legions with a more deadly creation.'

Stephen ran to the side of the fallen nazdarg, lifted him onto his shoulders and carried him to the passage through which the medical team had taken the casualties. Several stretcher bearers were already in position, waiting to carry the wounded away in the event of a further attack. 'Take him to Valsa,' he commanded, 'and do not let any other doctor treat him. She'll know what to do.'

The silence was eerie. The howls of the nazdargs had grown fainter and then had suddenly stopped. The outlaws strained their eyes and ears, but there was no sign of the enemy. Benedict beckoned to a short, sinewy man with skin like polished ebony. 'Go and spy on the enemy and report to me.' The man gave a sharp salute and vanished into the darkness. Minutes passed, the seconds ticking by like the beat of a slow pulse, but the spy did not return. The silence tested the nerve of the defenders, stretching them to breaking point. Benedict beckoned to Crispian, and together they went from company to company, whispering encouragements and strengthening the outlaws.

Crispian would never be Benedict's equal as fighter, but he had changed dramatically since arriving at the canyon. The self-doubt and torment had gone and he was full of hope. The years of rejection had left their mark on him, but already he moved with assurance among the people. As Dimrat's prisoner, he could only give empty speeches, full of fine ideals but impossible to fulfil. Dimrat tortured him with futility. Here, however, his dreams of a just and better world inspired the people and gave them hope and a vision of the future. Crispian was a king in waiting, and as he moved from group to group with Benedict, his words lifted the hearts of the outlaws and gave them courage and a dream worthy of any sacrifice.

The attack began in silence. Hideous shapes leaped from the tunnel entrance and sprang at the defenders. Even Benedict was shaken, but only for a moment. He vaulted onto a boulder and gave a great cry. 'For the Captain and freedom. Victory!' And he raced to meet the leader of the kilvarst hosts.

Joanna was tempted to run away, but fascination overcame her panic. The kilvarsts were terrible: smaller than the nazdargs, with overdeveloped shoulder and thigh muscles. One sprang at her. She aimed the gun clumsily and yanked the trigger back. *Bang!* The gun jerked in her hands, and the explosion made her ears sing. The bullet was diverted by the kilvarst's body armour, but it momentarily halted the monster's charge. Joanna used the advantage. She kicked upwards with all her strength and felt her foot collide with the monster's jaw. The kick was so savage that it lifted the kilvarst from the floor and snapped its neck like a twig, the impact sending a bolt of agony through Joanna's leg.

'Hope it's not broken,' she whimpered, and she leaned the weight of her body onto the injured limb. 'Ouch! It hurts like crazy.'

The kilvarst lay at her feet, its brutal eyes staring vacantly into space. Joanna wanted to vomit. 'It looks horrible,' she gasped. Its head was small, but its jaws were enormous, the lower fangs driven through the roof of its mouth by the force of her kick. The kilvarst did not have a nose, but there were two tiny airholes immediately below its eyes. The cranium had been replaced by a transparent dome, and the brain was visible beneath like an oyster without its shell.

The outlaws fought desperately, but they were slowly being driven back by the kilvarsts. More and more of the creatures swarmed into the passage and hurled themselves at the defenders. Their body armour made them immune to bullets, so the outlaws attacked them with knives and their bare hands. The kilvarsts did not have the human intelligence of the nazdargs, but they fought with fierce, animal cunning and ferocity.

Rumbold and Stephen guarded Benedict and Crispian, but even the giant's energy was beginning to wane. When Benedict's bullet had ricocheted from the kilvarst leader's body armour, it was Rumbold who had rescued him, smashing the creature's cranium dome with one blow. Benedict was exhausted, and one arm hung limp and useless, mauled in the jaws of a kilvarst. If words could win a battle, Crispian would have succeeded single-handed. He shouted encouragements to the outlaws until his voice croaked in his throat and turned to a raw whisper. His machete was bloodied, but he had no skill as a warrior. Stephen had saved him from injury and death on more occasions than either of them could remember.

'You're an ugly guardian angel,' croaked Crispian gratefully, 'but you do the job!' And he gave another wild swing of his machete at an attacking kilvarst. The blade swished past Stephen, and he had to leap to one side to avoid it.

'I might be an ugly guardian angel, but I don't want my wings clipped,' Stephen protested, and he felled the kilvarst with a sharp chop to the throat.

'Lift me up,' commanded Benedict. Rumbold lifted him onto his shoulders. 'Retreat! Retreat! Code: Operation Nemesis!'

A tall figure appeared in the mouth of the tunnel, surrounded by a bodyguard of giant nazdargs. 'Cut them off. Don't let one of them escape. And find the girl and bring her to me,' he commanded in a voice that dripped with poison.

'It's Dimrat,' screamed Joanna, and her voice gave her away.

112

'I'm glad that you recognise me. I was informed that I'd find you here, skulking among these outlaws. Come to me and I'll withdraw my forces immediately.'

Rumbold's voice rang out: 'Don't listen to him, Joanna. He's a liar! Run!'

She turned and limped away, ignoring the pain in her leg in her desperation to escape. Dimrat's bodyguard raced after her, but a huge nazdarg intercepted them, bounding from a passageway and launching himself at them like an avalanche. It was the nazdarg who had warned the outlaws of the arrival of the kilvarsts. His momentum was so great that the nazdargs of the bodyguard were hurled to the ground. The fight was fierce and brutal. Stephen and Rumbold raced to the assistance of the nazdarg, but the contest was one-sided. A fresh tide of kilvarsts and nazdargs swept into the cavern and poured into the fray.

'Keep them occupied, my darlings,' said Dimrat, 'while I catch the little sparrow and break her wings.' He ran into the passage after Joanna.

Joanna had memorised the canyon's labyrinth of passageways. She limped along as fast as she could, whimpering in pain. Large drops of perspiration slithered down her cheeks, her young body weeping in desperation. 'Must get to the sea,' she thought. 'I'll be able to swim away and escape. The Captain will save me.'

The passage sloped upwards. 'Got to go on. Can't stop!' she told herself, and she gritted her teeth against the agony of her leg. A wild howl echoed in the passage, and she could hear the distant scurrying of feet. 'Must go on. I must,' she groaned, and she forced herself to move faster, her sweat stinging her eyes and blurring her sight. The passage ended in a narrow ledge and beneath was the sea: wild, frothing waves dashing at the cliff and smashing in huge plumes of spray. She searched the ridge desperately, but there was no way of escape. She was trapped.

Dimrat appeared, his eyes striking at her like fangs. 'So you escaped from your cage, my sparrow, but not this time.'

Joanna levelled the gun at him and sighted him along the barrel. 'Stop where you are or I'll shoot you.'

Dimrat sauntered towards her. 'Shoot? Shoot? Your hands are shaking, Joanna. I think that you're afraid to shoot me.'

Joanna lowered the gun and dropped it at her feet. 'I can't,' she whispered. 'I can't kill you in cold blood.'

Dimrat laughed. It was a cold, harsh sound that hit Joanna like a slap. 'Too weak, Joanna, to pull the trigger and end a monster's life?'

The airship floated over the edge of the canyon. Joanna was suddenly hopeful and her face lit with joy. 'The Captain! The Captain's here!'

Dimrat followed the direction of her gaze and looked puzzled. 'I can see nothing, Joanna. Only a grey and empty sky.'

'But the sky isn't grey, and the Captain's airship is . . .'

Snarling kilvarsts leaped from the tunnel and dashed towards her, jaws wide and eyes mad with fury. Joanna stepped back in panic, lost her balance and toppled from the ledge.

The thunder of the waves drowned her scream.

19

Victory

Dimrat's élite bodyguard was slain, but the nazdarg was fatally wounded in the attack. Rumbold and Stephen did their best to protect him, shielding him from the jaws of the kilvarsts and the weapons of the nazdarg storm-troopers. Benedict regrouped the outlaws and attempted to rescue them, driving a wedge through the enemy, but he was quickly surrounded and the attack turned into a frenzied rout, his warriors toppling around him like a flimsy dyke of wood before a raging sea. For a moment, his eyes met Rumbold's.

'You must retreat, Benedict,' cried the giant, his face as stern as a commandment. 'There's nothing you can do for us here!'

'To the passages,' Benedict commanded, 'or all is lost,' and he stumbled from the fight, tears spattering his cheeks like blood.

Rumbold stumbled and struggled to his feet again. He saw Stephen fall and tried to save him, but he was beaten back by a charge of kilvarsts and nazdargs. He was stronger than any of them, crushing them as a bull elephant does a pack of hyenas, but his strength was almost gone and his breath was coming in great feverish gasps.

The sound began as a whisper and grew quickly to a terrible roaring, a torrent of screams and howls that gushed along the entrance tunnel and crashed into the cavern like a giant wave. Nazdargs and kilvarsts pelted from the tunnel mouth, their jaws flecked with foam and eyes rolling in terror. Madness afflicted them. They dashed themselves against rocks, tore at one another with fanged jaws, rolled on the ground as if their flesh burned with fire, or, numb with dread, lay twitching on their backs, their eyes frosted and iced with fear. And behind them, his eyes flaming with terrible light, strode the Captain, the legions of Dimrat stampeding before him like zebras stalked by a pride of lions. His skin was ablaze, and lightning streaked across his body like arteries of white hot fire. He was a man like any other man, but in him raged the energies that lit the stars and flung the planets into space. Rumbold staggered and fell before him, his soul bursting open in a flood of joy, and Stephen cried out: 'Father!'

The Captain lifted the dying nazdarg from beneath a pile of corpses and power poured into him like a river of light. The nazdarg's body became as transparent as glass, every bone and organ visible, his heart twittering like a bird in the cage of his chest. Then the light faded and the nazdarg was himself again.

'You shall be called Joshua because I have taken you from the jaws of death and given you life,' said the Captain, and he placed him on his feet. Joshua's wounds had vanished and he was healed, but before he could thank the Captain, he had swept after the nazdargs and kilvarsts, his presence burning them like acid.

*   *   *

The sea closed over Joanna and pulled her under. She struggled against it, kicking with her legs, but she was seized in the grip of a current and could not break free. Mad with fear of the Captain, the kilvarsts threw themselves after her and sank into the sea, trails of air bubbles plotting their progress downwards. The sun was no more than a blur of gold, its light drowned in the inky darkness of the ocean. Joanna's ears rang with the low pounding of the surf as it punched its white-knuckled fists against the cliff. She held her breath and fought the current, her lungs burning and sparks exploding in her eyes, and suddenly she was no longer sinking but rising, and strange music filled her ears. Her head burst from the sea, the stale air shrieking from her lungs. She breathed deeply—huge, gulping mouthfuls of air that smelled of salt and sea and sky, and something else: a warm, fishy twang. Bottle-nosed dolphins danced about her, angels winged with spray, singing to one another like choristers in a cathedral choir. Here, though, there was no nave or high altar, but the ocean and a sky fluted with clouds.

The dolphins' song turned to pictures in Joanna's mind, and she was no longer a girl but a dolphin speeding through the twilight kingdoms of the ocean. She explored continents buried beneath silent seas, visited magical cities of coral and meadows of sand sown with pearl, and hung suspended above underwater gardens, watching tiny fish in tropical plumage floating like birds in an aquamarine sky. And then the song ended and she was a girl again, riding the switchback waves in a dangerous sea.

A large female dolphin rubbed her short beak gently against Joanna's shoulder and uttered a series of squeals and high-pitched screams. The sounds turned into pictures and each picture became a word: 'Come, for we have been sent to carry you across the ocean.'

'Where are we going?' asked Joanna, but there was no reply from the dolphin.

'Cling to my dorsal fin,' she commanded. Joanna obeyed, and soon the land was merely a shadow against the distant sky.

The voyage passed like a dream. Joanna could understand the language of the dolphins and shared their joy, but their minds were alien to her. They loved and laughed and sang and felt pain and sorrow as we do, but there was no desire for conquest. They were content to be themselves and desired nothing except the company of others and the wild, exhilarating joy of the sea. Joanna listened, probing their intelligence, but they were a mystery to her.

A blunt-headed Risso's dolphin nudged her with his snout. 'Surf upon my back and I will teach you the magic of the sea.' Joanna clambered onto his back and stood shakily to her feet. The pain in her leg had gone, leaving only a slight discomfort. At first he moved sedately, but as Joanna grew accustomed to the motion his speed increased, the change of tempo in his muscles throbbing through her feet and legs. She balanced on his back like a dancer, or if his movements threatened to toss her into the sea, she crouched and clung to his dorsal fin, digging her toes into his light grey skin. But for all her skill, she was no match for him. A sudden twist or leap would cast her from his back, and then she would try again, the wind and spray in her face and a warm sun caressing her skin and taking the chill from her body. She laughed and whooped with joy, and only the present was important to her: an olive-skinned girl befriended by the gypsies of the sea. Her heart pounded, her eyes shone and she was full of glory.

Joanna smelled the land before she saw it, a faint signature of fragrance like the perfume of an old friend. The sun fell towards the west and the land rose to meet it, clambering above the skyline and slowly filling the horizon.

A coral reef circled the island like a defensive wall, and beyond, Joanna could see spouts of water shooting into the sky. The dolphins raced towards the reef, the sea about Joanna boiling and writhing with their speeding bodies.

'Down,' commanded the dolphin, and she sat on his back, her hands clutching his fin and her legs gripping his body. Breakers rolled lazily towards the reef, lifted themselves slowly as if encumbered by a terrible weight of water and dashed themselves to pieces on the stubborn coral. The dolphin, with Joanna on his back, leaped the reef in one majestic, heart-stopping moment, the surf thundering beneath and blizzards of spray driving into them. They hit the water on the far side, dipped under in a graceful dive and surfaced.

A deep, clear lagoon stretched out before Joanna and whales lolled and frolicked in it like giant cattle in a meadow of blue, their calves beside them. They were huge and beautiful and as ancient as the world, and their voices boomed in her ears like an organ recital. 'Welcome, little one. We were told of your coming.'

Day was dying and the sky was awash with colour. The whales swam slowly towards her, the vast spatulas of their tails beating the sea to a white froth. Joanna surfed among them on the back of her friend, the Risso dolphin, awed by their size and majesty.

'Come, daughter of the land, the lord is here and desires to meet you,' they cried, and a path of open water appeared, their grey bodies lining either side of it like menhirs marking an ancient processional way.

Joanna moved slowly along the path the whales had made for her. She saw every kind of whale, from bulbous-headed pilot whales to the most feared and dangerous predators of the sea: the sleek, black killer whales. Their voices were silent now, and their eyes inscrutable, waiting with the patience of earth's oldest intelligence. The sea was no longer blue, but decked in banners and streamers of colour borrowed from the tropical sunset. Mystery hung in the air around her like incense, clogging her soul with wonder and filling her with a joyful kind of dread.

'It's like a ceremony,' Joanna thought, 'but who is this lord of the sea? Why does he want to see me?'

At first Joanna mistook the blue whale for a

submerged reef, a dark shadow lurking beneath the surface of the water, but as she drew nearer, she saw his broad head, tiny dorsal fin and the wide 'V' of his tail. The whale was huge, at least a hundred and forty feet in length, and it bestrode the path before her, forbidding her progress. At the sight of the whale, the dolphin grew nervous and his body trembled.

'It is he,' said the dolphin, 'but I am afraid lest he look upon me with his eyes and I perish.'

The sea stirred and foamed, and the whale breached the surface, the spray from its blow scattering across Joanna like gems of liquid light.

'Perish! Perish!' echoed the whale in a voice as deep and as beautiful as the ocean. 'Perish! Yes, there have been those who have perished when I have looked upon them, and I have sunk worlds with a toss of my tail, but you need not fear me. Come closer, brother, and let me bless you.' The dolphin lost his fear of the lord of the sea and nuzzled up to him.

'Is it true, then,' said the dolphin, 'that you are the father of all who dwell in the sea?'

'It is true, my son.'

'And did you not raise the dry land from the sea and scatter all manner of creatures upon it?'

'You have said truly, my son.'

'Then even if I were to die this day from the glance of your eyes, I would not turn aside, for to see you is better than life itself.'

Joanna was humbled by the whale's size. One eye was hidden and the eye that surveyed her was wild and joyful, brimming with life.

'Come here, little one!' he commanded, and his huge tail beat on the sea and threw Joanna from her perch on the dolphin. The sea closed over her head, and for seconds she hung suspended below the surface, the whale jewelled in the gold of the setting sun. She rose spluttering to the surface, but her reprimand was silenced by his eye.

'Little sister, your kind have hunted us to extinction. Your greed is so vast and cruel that you could kill the seas and turn the land to dust. You're parasites—tiny, strutting creatures who foul the earth and boast of your intelligence. Beware! Knowledge without wisdom has made you fools—dangerous, reckless fools—who govern by greed and plunder the garden of the earth. We are your elder brothers and sisters, for we were here before you, but you live as if you only are important. Remember! One Father gave us life, and one universe holds us in its cradle.'

'But we're not all bad,' protested Joanna. 'Some of us ...'

But before Joanna could finish her defence, the whale spoke, his voice roaring like a stormy sea. 'A new menace threatens us all. Here on this island you will be told how to bring the colour back to the land. A woman and a friend await you. Go, for they are waiting. He reared out of the water and breathed upon her, his breath filling her with strength and courage. 'Thus have I blessed you,' he said, and his voice rose like a tempest. 'Beware of the fangs of Filcheeth and the Lake of Dreams.'

A cry carried to her across the lagoon: 'Joanna!' Two figures stood on the beach, and one was a giant.

'Take me to the beach ... quickly,' commanded Joanna. Never had the dolphin known such joy. He had seen the lord of the sea—and lived! He leaped in the air, Joanna crouched on his back, and danced across the mirror-smooth surface of the lagoon to the shore.

'I will remember this day tomorrow, and the day after, and for ever,' cried the dolphin.

'So will I,' whispered Joanna.

Darkness had fallen, and flocks of stars grazed in the meadows of night. Joanna turned and saw the whales silhouetted against the sky, and in their midst,

121

the lord of the sea. She knew then how she would spend the rest of her life.

'His eye was familiar,' she murmured, and she groped to remember where she had seen it before.

20

The Island

Rumbold splashed through the surf and lifted Joanna from the back of the dolphin.

'You must be starving,' he said.

'Now I come to think of it, I am,' she said, 'but you'd better introduce me to your friend.'

The woman was slender, with skin as brown as a coconut shell. Her eyes were sharp and inquisitive, but it was too dark for Joanna to identify their colour. In the twilight, the woman appeared young and beautiful, but as Joanna approached, she saw that her face was wrinkled and the long, black velvet of her hair was patched with silver.

'Welcome, Joanna!' said the woman. 'I believe that you've met my daughter, Martha.' The voice was clear and direct, matching the honesty of her eyes.

'Adriana!' exclaimed Joanna in surprise, and she studied the woman closely. She seemed as sharp and bright as a diamond. It wouldn't be easy to fool her, she thought.

'Don't gawk at me, girl.'

'I'm sorry, but you look like your brother.'

'That's my misfortune,' she replied curtly, 'but our looks are the only thing that we have in common. Rumbold tells me that you've been chosen by the Captain to bring colour back to the land.'

'Yes!'

'In that case you're going to need my help. Dimrat's hard to beat.' Her face softened. 'Your clothes are sodden and you must be very hungry.'

'Yes, I am,' she replied, but her curiosity was stronger than her appetite. 'How did you get here, Rumbold? Did we win the battle?'

'One question at a time, Joanna,' protested Rumbold with a chuckle, and as they walked to Adriana's house he told his story. 'The battle was going badly until the Captain's arrival.'

'The Captain?' said Joanna in surprise.

'Yes! He appeared when Dimrat's legions were beginning to get the upper hand. Benedict had retreated and was going to flood the passages, but before he could do so the Captain arrived and drove the kilvarsts and nazdargs from the canyon.'

'How did he do it?'

'That's the most remarkable part of the story. He came alone and had no weapon. His presence was sufficient to drive the enemy mad with fear and panic. You should have seen them. At the sight of him, the nazdargs dropped their weapons and ran and the kilvarsts squealed with terror and threw themselves around as if they had been burned by napalm. They went crazy.'

'What of Dimrat?'

'I don't know what happened to him. He followed you along the passage, but when I reached the ledge above the sea there was no sign of him. He'd vanished.'

'He was on the ledge when I fell into the sea.'

Rumbold frowned. 'He certainly wasn't there when I arrived. The ledge was empty.'

'How did you manage to get here?'

'I dived from the ledge and searched the sea for you. The currents are deadly just below the cliff and there was little chance of finding you alive, but I had to be certain. I was exhausted from the fight and was soon struggling for my life.' A shadow passed across the giant's face at the memory. He was silent for a few seconds before he resumed the story. 'And then about thirty metres or so in front of me I saw a shelf of rock below the surface of the sea. They say that a man who's lost in the desert often imagines that he sees an oasis, only to discover that it's a mirage. I wondered if the shelf of rock was real or an hallucination. I struggled towards it. Then, without warning, the rock lifted from the sea and a deep voice carried to me across the water: 'Be still, O waves, and cease you roaring angry sea.' Instantly the ocean became as quiet as a pond.

'An enormous blue whale swam towards me. 'Do not be afraid, my son,' he called, 'for she whom you seek is found and you will soon meet her. Come, sit upon my back and we will journey together, for I have much to say to you.'

'He was the lord of the sea,' exclaimed Joanna, recognising him from the description immediately.

Rumbold nodded. 'Yes, Joanna, he brought me to this island to await your arrival. It seems that I'm to be your guardian.' A gleam of humour sparkled in his eyes. 'He thought you needed someone to protect you. He wasn't sure you could look after yourself.'

Instead of the defiance Rumbold expected, Joanna's reply was humble. 'He was right. I do need your help. I don't think I could succeed by myself.'

'That's my home,' said Adriana, interrupting their conversation. She had listened silently to Rumbold and Joanna and was beginning to like the girl.

Joanna saw lights twinkling through the trees, and there before her was a small cottage surrounded by low thatched buildings. She could smell the sweet perfume of flowers and hear the musical tinkle of water, a refreshing sound in the balmy heat of a tropical night. The pool was so clear that even in the darkness Joanna could see fish moving like shadows in its depths. A spring ruffled the surface at one end, but for most of its length it was as smooth and clear as glass, reflecting the stars and the gold of the moon.

Joanna's hair was matted, and the sun had dried her legs and arms, leaving a film of white salt on her skin. Adriana read the longing in her face. 'Dinner will be in fifteen minutes. Why not have a swim in the pool, Joanna? You can change into some of my clothes.'

Joanna smiled gratefully at the woman. 'Thanks!'

Adriana entered the cottage and beckoned to Rumbold to follow. The giant fell to his knees, twisted his mighty body through the narrow opening of the door and disappeared within.

As soon as they were gone, Joanna crouched down and splashed the water with her hand. 'It feels beautiful,' she whispered and quickly slipped out of her wet clothes. She jumped into the pool and laughed with ecstacy as the cool water tickled her limbs and washed the salt and perspiration from her body. Shoals of tiny fish scattered from her, flashing silver in the moonlight. In the trees, the long-legged crickets serenaded her, their song accompanied by the distant music of the sea. Joanna swam and dived and thrashed the water with her arms, celebrating her youth and the wild joy of living.

A shadow passed across the moon and darkened the pool. Joanna looked up, but instead of a ragged patch of cloud, she saw the airship. The darkness quivered and a figure appeared, his face shining like molten tar. Without saying a word, he stooped and placed a bundle on the grass. Joanna hauled herself out of the pool and ran towards the Captain, but he vanished, leaving her backpack on the ground behind him. She looked up, searching the night for the airship, but it had gone.

Opening the backpack, she found a brief note: 'My dear Joanna, you'll need your belongings. Enjoy your swim. I've enclosed a large bath towel. You'll need it on the island. My blessing: The Captain.' Joanna flung the towel around her, pummelled her body dry and then searched the backpack for a change of clothes and her wide-toothed comb. Dressed in a loose-fitting blouse and a brightly patterned skirt, she knocked on the cottage door and entered. Rumbold and Adriana looked round in amazement.

'Where did you get those clothes?' asked Adriana. 'They certainly don't belong to me.'

'The Captain gave them to me,' she replied, and a deep silence filled the room.

The days that followed were heady, dreamy days of sun, sea and bird song in the shaded aviary of the forest. On her first morning, Joanna was awakened by the happy voices of children. Springing from her bed in a whitewashed attic room, she had run nimbly to the window and looked out. Boys and girls were tumbling from the thatched buildings and sitting cross-legged on the rich green carpet of grass surrounding the pool. A tall, skinny boy with a thatch of straw-coloured hair was organising them into neat rows.

'There'll be no breakfast until you're all sitting down properly,' he shouted, lifting his voice above the medley of children's babble. In an instant, the children became as ordered as a regiment of soldiers. The door beneath Joanna's window opened and Adriana appeared, wheeling a trolley loaded with fruit, freshly-baked bread and a huge churn of goats' milk.

That was Joanna's introduction to the orphans. She was never quite sure how the children arrived on the island. When she pressed them to disclose their secret, they grew silent and smiled at her mysteriously. 'We've promised not to tell,' they said, and they

126

scanned the blue sky with dreaming eyes like sleep walkers.

Adriana was equally evasive. 'Secrets are like locked doors, Joanna. They must not be forced open.' Joanna had grown to like the woman. She was frightening, and her tongue was as tart as a lemon, but hidden beneath the spikes was a kind and generous person. The orphans adored her and called her 'mother'.

In the evening, on the eighth day of their stay, Adriana summoned Joanna and Rumbold into her cottage. 'There's no use beating about the bush,' she said abruptly 'The holiday is over, and you must fulfil your mission. Sit down at the table.'

Joanna and Rumbold obeyed, turning their faces towards Adriana expectantly. She spread a map before them. 'Here is Dimrat's House of Many Rooms,' she said, and she stabbed her finger at a point in the south-eastern corner of the map. 'The grey smog comes from a door in the basement of his house. You must pass through the door, take the key from its owner and close it. If you succeed, the colours will return to the land. If you fail, there is no hope for any of us.'

Rumbold studied the map carefully, his face troubled. 'I remember little of the House of Many Rooms. We escaped from it in gunships and found refuge in the mountains when I was only a child.' His finger traced the contours of the map and he looked startled. 'It's situated in the fens of Filcheeth. No wonder Dimrat's lair has never been found. What does the proverb say? "He who dares the fens of Filcheeth hates his life." No one has ever passed across the fens and returned to tell the story.'

'I have,' said Adriana.

Rumbold looked at her in surprise. 'When? How?' 'When I refused to help my brother with his experiments, he kept me a prisoner in his House of Many Rooms. I escaped across the fens of Filcheeth.'

'Alone?' asked Rumbold.

'No! My husband was with me.' She saw the question in their eyes.

'His grave is in the fens of Filcheeth.'

'I'm sorry,' whispered Joanna.

Adriana's face was sad and haunted by memories. She squared her shoulders and spoke, breaking the spell of silence that had fallen on the room. 'There is a way. Look!'

The fens of Filcheeth were vast flatlands that stretched from the south-easterly seaboard deep into the interior of the land. A path had been drawn across the marshes, and compass references and descriptions of the terrain had been written on either side of it in small, tidy handwriting. Adriana followed the path with her finger.

'This is the route. If you stray from it, you're as good as dead.' The path ended on the shores of a lake. 'Here are Dimrat's headquarters,' she said, pointing at a small island that scowled from the centre of the lake like the pupil of an eye. 'There are still creatures hidden in the marshes who remember the time when the fens were the haunt of rare birds and wild flowers. It was a beautiful place once, and even now, Dimrat has not been able to ruin it completely. You can have this map and my compass. Follow the path and you'll reach Dimrat's House of Many Rooms. Only the Captain can help you then!'

'But how do we get back to the land?' enquired Joanna.

'In the same way that you came here . . . by sea!'

*   *   *

The inflatable danced across the sea, its powerful outboard engine thrusting it forward towards the distant skyline. Joanna had slept fitfully the night before, her sleep troubled by dreams of the ordeal that lay before her. But now, lulled by the song of the wind and the gentle lapping of the waves, she dozed contentedly, her head pillowed in the circle of her arms. Rumbold sat in the stern of the boat, one hand resting on the tiller and the other holding a large marine compass. A pack of killer whales surged through the sea on either side of the inflatable, their upright dorsal fins slicing through the water like knife blades.

The land merged into the sea. The only warnings of its presence were the grey mist that slithered across the skyline and the flocks of grey gulls that patrolled the sky above it. Rumbold sniffed the wind, his nostrils flaring, and smelled the dank, musty odour of the marshes. One moment the sky and sea were blue, and the next, the world turned grey and only Joanna retained her colours.

The killer whales squealed in alarm, their black bodies and white markings turned suddenly grey by the evil magic of the land. The leader of the pack, a lean male of about thirty feet in length, sped to the side of the boat and 'spy-hopped', his broad, paddle-shaped flippers beating the waves in anguish. Joanna awoke and saw his grey head towering above the inflatable. She saw the grey sky and breathed the rank, stagnant air of the marshes.

'Go now,' she commanded, 'and may the sea carry me to you again.' Their voices uttered the sounds of farewell, and the pack turned and fled from the 'grey' into the blue, sunlit prairies of the ocean.

The sea grew shallow and choked with weeds, and long grey eels twisted in the water below the boat. 'We should see the mouth of the River Fengrief very shortly,' said Rumbold, his voice hushed and sober in the brooding silence.

Reeds bristled along the shoreline like a wall of

spears, forbidding entry. Beyond, the marsh awoke and waited. Their boat moved slowly onwards, the rhythmic chug, chug of its outboard engine echoing eerily across endless mud flats.

A sudden break in the reed wall marked the opening of the River Fengrief. The river flowed without joy or melody, but sulked across the fens of Filcheeth to the sea. The rudder turned and a tiny wave lifted the prow of the boat. Ranks of reed and gnarled willow closed in about Joanna and Rumbold, and when they turned, the ocean had disappeared and a wall of mist barred their escape.

21

The Fens of Filcheeth

Writhing snakes of mist crawled across their path, and a grey sky pressed down on them resentfully. Joanna and Rumbold had left the river and were trudging along a narrow embankment that bridged the marshes of Filcheeth. On either side of them, the marsh land gurgled and spluttered, a treacherous sea of mire that heaved and trembled as if a huge creature moved beneath its surface. The fens of Filcheeth fed on the carrion of rotting trees and vegetation, and its breath stank of decay. The only lives that thrived and multiplied here were the floating bladderworts and the buzzing mosquito swarms: tiny, ravenous vampires mad for blood. They attacked Joanna and Rumbold without pity.

'How long will it take to cross the marshes?' inquired Joanna impatiently, brushing mosquitoes from her face with the back of her hand. 'These mosquitoes are driving me crazy.'

Rumbold stopped and pointed at the map. 'I estimate we're about two-thirds of the way across. There are no landmarks, so it's difficult to be absolutely sure, but we've been walking for over six hours.'

Joanna looked at the display on her digital watch. 'Six hours and forty-seven minutes to be precise. I wish the scenery would change. These marshy flatlands are terribly boring to look at.'

'According to Adriana's map, there's a lake ahead of us. We'll camp there,' said Rumbold. 'The water will be okay to drink if we boil it. We might even be able to catch a large pike or carp to eat. Do you feel hungry?'

'Starving!'

The grey sun hung low in the west by the time they reached the lake. It was fed by a river and several smaller streams, and it stretched from the eastern wall of the embankment deep into the marsh. Gnarled, but still majestic, white willows grew along its banks and gardens of lilies, frogbit, crowfoot and other aquatic plants blossomed in its shallows. During their trek, Joanna and Rumbold had only seen stunted shrubs and bushes sprouting from the embankment, but here tall birch trees stood sentry and the occasional oak and squat hawthorn spread their branches to the sky, their leaves murmuring in a gentle conversation. The lake was clear and clean and shoals of fish moved lazily in its depths.

'Come here!' said Rumbold, his voice urgent and excited. Joanna ran to him. 'Look!' He pointed to the water immediately below the embankment.

'It's a boat, but we'll never be able to use it. It's rotten with age and half submerged.'

'I know that, but it does mean that people visited this lake once.'

'It doesn't feel so . . .' Joanna searched for words.

'Diseased?' said Rumbold helpfully.

'Yes, diseased. Did you feel it as well?'

'Yes, I did. Here there's a different atmosphere. The place feels healthy. I wasn't looking forward to camping in the marshes, but this is the ideal site. If you put up your tent and start a fire, I'll catch some fish. We'll eat well tonight,' said Rumbold cheerfully.

The Captain had given Joanna a dome tent. It was easy to erect and very spacious. She unrolled her mattress and sleeping bag, and then, clutching her waterproof matches and cooking set, crawled through the tent's zip door. Rumbold sat on the embankment fishing. He had no rod or net, but dangled a length of nylon line into the water below him. Joanna was about to speak when he put a warning finger over his lips and hissed: 'Be quiet!' His body was tense and his eyes alert. The line gave a sudden pull and the slack disappeared. With a quick jerk of his wrist, he hooked the fish and pulled it struggling to the bank. 'It's a plump carp,' he said, and he held it proudly for Joanna to see.

'Did you see that?' asked Joanna, pointing urgently. Rumbold looked in the direction of her finger. A flurry of ripples troubled the water, but there was no sign of fish, or bird, or any other creature.

'What was it?'

'I don't really know, but I thought I saw a large shadow just below the surface of the lake and two bright eyes staring at us.'

'Don't worry about it. It must have been a fish. I've seen some big pike in the lake.'

Rumbold thrust a large, juicy worm on his barbed hook and cast the line into the lake. *Splash!* Joanna watched the worm sink, its wriggling body magnified by the water, and saw a sleek shadow rise and speed towards it. The line twanged taut like an overstretched guitar string, and the hooked fish sprang from the water and twisted against the pull of the line, its tail thrashing the air in fury. Rumbold anticipated the ploy and lowered his arm to reduce the strain on the slender nylon thread.

'You don't fool me, you beauty,' he yelled, and he played the fish cunningly, allowing it to exhaust itself in desperate leaps, dives and long, futile runs. Soon, however, it weakened and lay limply on the surface of the lake, its tail beating the water listlessly in defeat. 'We'll be eating well tonight, Joanna.' Rumbold sniffed and smacked his lips. 'A monster brown trout tastes better than a salmon. Light the fire for a fresh fish barbecue.'

Several times that evening Joanna imagined that she saw a huge shape skim below the surface of the lake, but she could never be certain. The creature, if it was indeed a creature, was stealthy and cleverly camouflaged, keeping itself hidden from their prying eyes.

The fire burned brightly and the dry wood spluttered and crackled, showering the night with fountains of sparks. The flames danced a wild rumba and then, exhausted by the effort, sank down to rest in a bed of smouldering, white hot embers. Rumbold covered each fish in a mould of mud and laid them in the embers to bake.

'Delicious!' whispered Joanna as the aroma of sizzling flesh scented the night. The glow of the fire, the sweet smell of cooking fish and the lullaby of the trees lifted the oppression of the marshes and soothed her spirit. She lay on her back with her arms behind her head and sang one of the Captain's songs. She was surprised that the melody and lyric came so easily to her memory. As her husky, tuneful voice skipped across the lake, the grey vanished from the night and the stars swarmed above her like shoals of silver fish.

Rumbold sat upright and rubbed his eyes. 'Am I dreaming? I can see the stars. The grey has vanished.'

'You're not dreaming, Rumbold. I'm singing one of the Captain's songs, and it seems to be driving the grey away from this place.'

Joanna saw a head lift above the surface of the lake and two sorrowful eyes gazed at her unblinkingly, the firelight sparkling in them. Speech gurgled in her mind like water: 'I have watched and waited for this hour. The promise is true: a song will light the stars and paint the world with colour.'

'Look!' she yelled, pointing at the creature, but her voice alarmed it and it sank into the lake.

'What?'

'I saw a strange creature, and its voice spoke in my mind.'

'You're imagining it, Joanna. It was probably a fish rising for a fly, or maybe the reflection of the fire on the water. Let's eat!'

The fish were delicious. Joanna flaked the meat from the sharp bones and munched slowly, savouring the taste. She glanced at Rumbold and saw the pleasure on his face as he ate. As a child, she had imagined that giants were crude and greedy fellows, tearing at their food with rotten teeth and belching loudly, but Rumbold ate with dignity. His eyes were mysterious and glowed softly in the firelight. Joanna never questioned him about his past. She had tried, but he refused to answer her.

Rumbold turned and smiled at her. 'There are better things to stare at than me, Joanna.'

'I was just wondering about you. Why are you afraid to tell me about your past?'

Rumbold looked uncertain and opened his mouth as if to speak.

'Why?' queried Joanna, her eyes searching Rumbold's face for answers.

'I can't, Joanna.' His eyes were as desperate as a trapped animal's. 'One day, one day, I may be able to tell you, but not here, not tonight. If you have any respect for me, never ask that question again.'

A shadow fell between them. 'I think I'll go to sleep now,' whispered Joanna, and she caressed the giant's shoulder with her fingertips. 'Goodnight! I'm sorry if I hurt you.'

'You didn't hurt me, Joanna. The hurt was inflicted long ago. Goodnight, and may the Captain give you sleep!'

As Joanna lay in her sleeping bag, she could see the silhouette of Rumbold through the skin of her tent. He sat beside the fire as motionless as a statue. The giant was her friend and he cared for her, but she didn't really know him. He was as mysterious and remote as the distant stars. A duet of lapping water and quivering leaves sang her to sleep, and in her dreams she saw mournful eyes gazing at her from the lake.

The sun rose, accompanied by a chorus of bird song, and awoke Joanna from her sleep. At first she thought she was back in her tidy Brixton bedroom, but the faint flapping of the tent and the bright, orange glow of the sunlight on its walls reminded her of her whereabouts. She snuggled into the cosy warmth of her sleeping bag and listened to the music of the dawn chorus. A fact slowly registered in her mind: 'There should be no colour and song in this land. What's happening?'

Joanna unzipped her sleeping bag, pulled on her clothes and crawled through the tent door. A ragged hole had been torn in the grey shroud above the lake and surrounding marshland, revealing a cloudless blue sky. 'It was my singing that did it. The Captain's songs must have power over the grey,' she thought, and her heart leaped with excitement.

The lake was as clear as glass, and its banks were carpeted with rose pink balsams and yellow marigolds. Thick crops of Michaelmas daisies grew on the sides of the embankment, their white flowers fluttering together like drifts of snow. The water immediately in front of Joanna was clear, but some metres to her left, pink flowering rushes enclosed secret gardens of white and yellow water lilies, pink bistort and the dainty white flowers of the frogbit. A brown otter splashed into the water, a 'V' of ripples tracing its progress across the lake, and a blue-winged kingfisher darted from the reeds, a silver minnow sparkling in its beak.

Rumbold lay asleep near the ashes of the fire. A grey heron paddled the sky above him, and its shadow floated across his face. He stirred and murmured but did not awake. Seven fat trout lay in a line near his feet.

'I won't wake him,' Joanna thought. 'I'll light the fire and cook the trout myself.' She rolled the fish into moulds of mud as she had seen Rumbold do the night before, lit the fire and placed them carefully in the embers.

The early sun danced on the lake and its water swished and splashed in welcome. Joanna slipped out of her clothes and slid down the embankment into its crystal depths. 'Ooh,' she gasped as the cold water chilled her limbs, but the effort of swimming and the heat of the sun on her back soon warmed her body. Marsh warblers skimmed the surface of the lake, fleeing upwards in a flutter of brown wings at the sight of her. Shoals of fish moved slowly through the water beneath her.

Words formed in Joanna's mind: 'Do not be afraid.' She saw a huge shadow rising from the depths of the lake towards her. 'Do not be afraid for I wish you no harm.'

Joanna was terrified. 'Dear God,' she pleaded, 'don't let it kill me.'

'Have no fear of death,' said the voice, 'for I come in friendship.'

136

A great, green head broke the surface of the lake next to Joanna, and she was looking into the protruding eyes of a giant frog, its brown irises flecked with gold. It croaked, and words splashed into Joanna's mind: 'I thank you, daughter, for bringing the colour back to my kingdom. I offer you my service and have left a gift for you.'

'A gift!' said Joanna in amazement.

'When you were asleep, I left trout beside your fire. I will guide you through the fens of Filcheeth.'

The frog, with Joanna clinging to its back, sprang from the lake onto the embankment. Rumbold awoke and leaped to his feet, a sword glittering in his hand. 'It's a friend,' yelled Joanna, her head appearing from behind the frog's shoulder. 'Don't harm it.' Rumbold gaped at the frog and girl in amazement and slowly lowered his sword. 'So much for your pike, Rumbold.'

The giant recovered his composure and gave Joanna his wry half smile. 'So, the frog princess returns. What does the creature want?'

'It's a "she", Rumbold. She came in the night and left the trout that are cooking in the embers. She's promised to guide us through the fens of Filcheeth.'

Rumbold looked at the frog, his eyes sharp and suspicious. 'How can you be sure we can trust this big lady?'

'Her heart is open to me. I can understand her thoughts. She doesn't want to harm us, Rumbold, but help us in our quest to stop the grey from killing the land. She is no creature or friend of Dimrat's.'

22

The Lake of Dreams

The powerful rear legs of the frog propelled her forward in a series of hops. Joanna and Rumbold trudged behind her through an evil landscape of gurgling, sucking bog. One slip, one careless step and they would be buried in a tomb of mud. The lake and the embankment were far behind them, and the land and sky had turned to grey. Dense clumps of Sphagnum moss hid traps of sinking mire, and water scorpions danced in stagnant pools. Sometimes they waded ankle deep in salty water, and, at such times, leeches clung to their skin and added to their misery. The only sounds were the slurping of mud and the drone of mosquitoes.

'How far before we reach the Lake of Dreams?' groaned Joanna.

'Not long now. A couple more miles perhaps and we'll be out of the fens.'

'Good riddance,' said Joanna with feeling.

They squelched through the mire in silence, enduring the trek with gritty determination. The frog touched minds with Joanna: 'In my youth, these fens were beautiful, home to rare birds, wild flowers and ducks, but they have grown hateful. We come to the most dangerous part of our journey: the fangs of Filcheeth.'

'The fangs of Filcheeth,' cried Joanna in alarm. 'The Captain warned me of this place.'

'So he should,' gurgled the frog, 'for those who pass between them seldom return.'

On either side of the path before them were fangs of sharpened rock. Rumbold drew his sword and its blade shimmered in the grey light. Joanna and

Rumbold followed the frog cautiously through the fangs of Filcheeth, their eyes alert and their bodies tensed for action. The air was chill and the mud reeked of decay. A broken tooth of rock lay beside the path.

'There's some writing on that rock,' whispered Joanna hoarsely. 'What does it say?'

Rumbold stooped over the stone and read the words: 'Here fell my beloved Jonathan. May he sleep in peace until the morning of the awakening.'

'I wonder who he was,' said Joanna sadly.

'I think you know,' replied Rumbold. 'Jonathan was Adriana's husband.'

'I wonder what happened to . . .' But before Joanna had time to finish the question, a terrible hissing arose from the marsh and whirlpools appeared on its surface, spinning downwards like whirling tops.

'We'll know soon enough,' said Rumbold grimly, and his face was fierce and his sword edge crackled with blue fire.

The frog shook with fear, but she did not desert them. The mire writhed and the hissing grew until the sky itself seemed to tremble. The attack came suddenly. Serpents uncoiled from the whirlpools and fanged jaws lashed out at them. Joanna ducked beneath the striking head of a serpent and fled along the narrow path. The path gave way beneath her and foul mud seized her ankles and began to drag her down.

'Help!' she shrieked.

'Don't struggle,' cried Rumbold as his sword leaped and danced in his hands like a bolt of savage lightning. A serpent struck at him. He dodged its fangs and severed its head, then pirouetted on his toes and killed another, his sword tip spiking its head between the eyes.

Joanna sank deeper into the bog, the black, sucking mud swallowing her slowly. 'Don't be long, Rumbold, or it will be too late,' she pleaded. The giant fought desperately, but he was trapped in a net of writhing serpents. His sword sang above their hissing, and its blade cut them down like reeds before a scythe, but the mire about him boiled with their bodies and there was no escape.

'Farewell, Joanna, and do not fail.' The frog's words were sad and melancholy, trembling in her mind like water lapping on a distant shore. Joanna saw the heavy-lidded eyes of the frog, and for a moment, their irises turned brown and flecks of gold danced in them like buttercups. 'Remember me, Joanna,' she croaked, and she sprang among the serpents, her powerful limbs thrashing out at them and her croaks echoing across the marsh. All of a sudden, the ring of serpents that encircled Rumbold lost interest in him and squirmed back into the mire after the frog. Their hissing receded, the only evidence of their presence the bubbles of mud that erupted from the mire.

Rumbold approached Joanna slowly, testing the path with his sword.

'Hurry,' she cried, as the black mud gripped her neck in a suffocating noose.

'If I hurry, Joanna, we'll both be dead.' Satisfied that the ground was firm enough to hold his weight, he knelt carefully on the path and stretched out his hand towards Joanna. She lifted her chin above the mire, and her hands searched desperately for the giant's arm.

She tried to speak, but mud gushed into her mouth and she choked.

'I've got you,' shouted Rumbold triumphantly, and a strong hand closed on her wrist and wrenched her from the bog. *Pop!* The mire surrendered her with a sound like a cork pulled from a bottle.

Joanna was so relieved to be alive she hardly noticed the stinking mud and slime that clung to her body. 'Thanks! Thanks!' she said, and because Rumbold was kneeling down, she threw her arms about his neck and kissed him. It was only then that she became aware of her appearance. 'I'm sorry. I'm really sorry.' She tried to brush the mud from Rumbold's clothes, but her efforts only served to spread it more widely.

Rumbold laughed. 'You look a real mess. Mud's supposed to be very good for the complexion. People pay big money for this sort of treatment at a beautician's.'

'They're welcome to it. I feel terrible.' Joanna's lips suddenly quivered and her eyes filled with tears. In the joy of her escape, she had forgotten the sacrifice of the frog. 'I don't feel much like laughing. The frog gave her . . . gave her . . .' But she was unable to complete the sentence.

'I know,' said Rumbold gently. 'Don't blame yourself for her death. She gave her life willingly. It was her gift to you. Remember that!'

'I'll try,' sobbed Joanna, and she felt ashamed of herself for crying in front of the giant. 'You're a tough girl,' she told herself, 'and tough girls don't bawl.' But try as she might, she could not stop her tears. 'I'm sorry, Rumbold, for crying like this. I feel like a little baby.'

'It takes a really big person to cry, Joanna. Even the Captain cries sometimes.'

'Does he really?'

'Yes! It's because he's so big that he cries.'

'What do you mean?'

'The Captain's much bigger than either of us, or, for that matter, anybody else in the world. He weeps with all those who suffer. His heart embraces the world.'

'His heart embraces the world,' echoed Joanna. 'That's very beautiful. It sounds like poetry.'

141

'It's the truth, Joanna.'

'Maybe,' she replied, 'but there are so many questions that I'd like him to answer.'

Without the frog to lead them, they relied on Adriana's compass and map. Joanna watched Rumbold as he drove the tip of his sword into the ground, testing the path before beckoning her to follow him along it.

'Your sword only appeared today. Where did you get it?' enquired Joanna.

'It's a long story, and we don't have time for long stories now. The Captain gave it to me. Now stop your questions and concentrate on the path. A second mud-bath could be fatal!'

Joanna and Rumbold glimpsed the Lake of Dreams through the thinning wall of reeds, an oval mere of water that watched them sullenly like a cyclops' eye. Soon they were standing on its banks, looking across a grey expanse of water to Dimrat's island.

'Have you noticed, Rumbold, that there are no reflections in this water?'

Rumbold nodded. 'Yes! It's some trickery of Dimrat's. You can be certain that he hasn't left his island unprotected.'

A bittern darted from the marshes and soared across the lake. They followed its flight and watched it hover above an outcrop of reeds.

'I can see a boat hidden in those reeds,' said Rumbold. 'The Captain sent the bird to guide us.'

'It could be coincidence, Rumbold, but whatever it is, I'm glad we don't have to swim to the island. The lake frightens me. I feel it's watching us.'

The only sound that disturbed the eerie silence of the lake was the muted *splash, splash* of their oars. The boat slid through the water, its prow hardly leaving a ripple on the surface. Dimrat's island grew closer, a dark shoreline covered with the stubble of broken trees, and behind Rumbold and Joanna, monsters of mist crawled across the fens of Filcheeth to the lake. Evil had awakened.

The water about them suddenly cleared and sparkled like a mirror. 'I don't like it,' growled Rumbold, and he rowed harder, but his strength was no match for the enchantment of the lake. The water burst into flames, and through the flames they could see huge figures.

'They're giants,' cried Joanna. 'What's happening?' But she received no reply from Rumbold. His eyes were wide with terror and phlegm flecked his lips.

Through the flames Joanna saw a range of mountains, their sharp summits mantled in a fleece of snow. In the foreground, thatched houses burned like torches, or collapsed inwards, exploding in vast columns of sparks. Packs of nazdargs hunted down the fleeing giants there, killing them without pity. Dimrat was their captain, his face aglow in the leaping flames. He laughed at the agony of the giants and taunted them as they died.

Joanna saw a young giant, only a child, hiding in a cleft of rock. His face was familiar. 'Oh, Rumbold,' she groaned, 'I understand now.' She saw the child's terrified eyes and saw his mouth open in a silent scream.

The scene changed. She saw the ruin of the giants' village: houses burned to smouldering grey ash and blackened bodies sprawled among the debris. A child wandered through the empty streets, his shoulders bowed with a load of guilt.

Rumbold sat as if paralysed, and the oars hung uselessly in his hands. Joanna prised them from him and began to row, the boat gliding through a haunted world of ghosts and nightmares. Wild beasts and monsters sprang at her from the depths of the lake, and a gigantic scorpion stalked her, its eyes gloating with greed and its tail leaking drops of poison into the water. Joanna struggled against the evil visions, concentrating her mind and will on rowing the boat to the island. The lake began to hiss and steam and Dimrat's face appeared in it, his eyes trapping Joanna as a stoat traps a rabbit with his stare. A cold draught of air fluffed the water into tiny waves and an evil voice breathed from the lake: 'Go no further, little sparrow. Step from the boat and drown in the water. Drown! Drown! Drown! Drown!'

'Captain,' Joanna cried, 'if you can help us, help us now.' Dimrat's reflection vanished and the lake shone with a soft, blue light. A figure walked towards them, growing taller and broader all the time, and his face filled the lake with light. He leaned over the giant and touched him gently on the brow, and then vanished.

Rumbold awoke from his enchantment and looked wildly about him. 'I dreamed I was chained in Dimrat's dungeons and the Captain freed me.' He seized the oars from Joanna and the boat surged across the lake towards the island.

The Captain had broken the power of the Lake of Dreams.

23

The House of Many Rooms

The lake was behind them, an unblinking eye rimmed by festering marshland, but still it watched them. Rumbold was shaking, his huge muscles twitching, his eyes unfocused, aghast. Joanna comforted him, her arms about his neck and her cheek against his. 'I understand now,' she whispered, 'I understand.'

And because she could think of no better thing to do, she kissed him.

All the tortured memories broke free and overwhelmed him. In his mind he was a child again watching the massacre of his family. Rolling over on his face, he clenched himself into a tight fist of tortured muscle and twisted limb and wept. Joanna wept with him.

Slowly the agony passed, the muscles unclenched, and Rumbold grew still. He sat up and looked steadily into Joanna's face, his gaze transparent, almost innocent. The shadows had gone from his eyes, leaving them clear and strangely beautiful.

'You look young!' said Joanna in surprise.

'I am,' said the giant, and then he corrected himself. 'I'm young as giants go. Just a youth.' He smiled at Joanna in that crooked, wistful way of his. Rumbold took a deep breath and looked around him. An evil fog clambered from the marshlands and crawled across the lake towards them, but the giant ignored it. This was the day of his rebirth. 'I'm free,' he said. 'The pain is still there. I don't think it will ever leave me, but I can talk about the past without . . .'

'Without what?' asked Joanna.

'Without . . .' Rumbold paused, groping for words. 'I can't explain. It's very difficult. It's almost as if Dimrat had power over me through the memories. Can you understand?'

'Yes, I think I can.'

'I'd torture myself, wondering if I did all that I could to save my family. I even felt guilty that I was alive and they were dead. I blamed myself somehow. Dimrat was always there, standing in my mind, accusing me, laughing at me. I don't know if I'm making sense to you. Am I?'

'Yes, you are,' said Joanna hesitantly. Rumbold's sudden openness had taken her by surprise. He'd always been so strong, hiding his thoughts and emotions from her. He was still the same reliable Rumbold, but now he was something more. She looked at him closely, her dark eyes bright and sharp. He had changed. A new and youthful Rumbold sat before her, cleansed of his guilt and memories. 'It's time to go,' she said, and she gave a soft sigh. 'I'm glad you're with me. I could never face this task without you.'

The fog drew nearer, stretching out its tentacles towards them.

A forest of tall trees had covered the greater part of the island before the coming of Dimrat, but these had been torn down and left to rot. Here and there a shattered tree remained, an epitaph to the murdered forest, with skeletal branches clawing at the sky in torment. Regiments of armoured termites feasted on the corpses of the trees, gorging themselves on rotten trunks and the tangled web of roots. The stench of death and decay was everywhere. In all the other places they had travelled, the name of Dimrat sounded like a note off key, but here it fitted perfectly.

Rumbold and Joanna walked in silence, oppressed by the utter desolation of their surroundings. 'Why did Dimrat want to kill the giants?' asked Joanna suddenly. The question had been nagging at her mind for some time.

'He made us,' said Rumbold, but before he could continue, Joanna interrupted him.

'Made you? You're so different from him. You're nothing like his other creatures.'

'I know we're different, but he did create us all the same. We were the first of his genetic experiments. He wanted to create a super-race, a sort of élite fighting corps who would obey him and murder for him. We were his secret weapon. He was going to unleash us on the land to conquer it, but the experiment was flawed. He made us huge and powerful, but he couldn't destroy the Maker's likeness in us. His experiment changed our bodies, but not our souls. The Maker touched us, and all the ingenuity of Dimrat couldn't change that. We were more than beasts. We were men with the nobility of men. Dimrat could never take that from us.'

'Why didn't he kill you when he first discovered his mistake?'

'It was too late then. We were too big and intelligent to control. He had no alternative but to let us go, but we were always an offence to him. He looked at us and heard the Maker laughing at him. It was only when he'd created creatures who'd do his bidding without protest that he felt strong enough to attack us. You know the rest of the story.'

Joanna reached out and held the giant's hand. 'Dimrat has done one good thing in his life, anyway.'

'What's that?' asked Rumbold in alarm.

'You!' said Joanna, looking into the giant's face. 'He created you!' But further conversation was silenced by the appearance of the House of Many Rooms.

Windows of all shapes and sizes stared blankly across the plain towards them. The house had no symmetry or beauty. Wall, roof and chimney were slung together randomly; the brickwork and masonry were covered in a film of grime and filth. The house was a monument to the obscenity of Dimrat's spirit, an abscess on the face of the world.

Joanna wanted to run away. 'If only I were back home with Dad and Mum,' she thought, but she was a prisoner. The Lake of Dreams cut off her escape as effectively as any prison door. There was no alternative but to go on. 'I'm scared,' she said in a frightened whimper of a voice. 'I wish . . . I wish I'd never agreed to come on this crazy mission. I was stupid to agree.' The house challenged her perception of herself. Its ugliness seemed to reach into her soul, pouring contempt on all her efforts and dreams, mocking her, making her feel worthless and insignificant.

'The Captain never makes a mistake, Joanna. He chose you, and if he did that you can be sure he knows exactly what he's doing. You're the best person for the mission.'

'Do you really believe that, Rumbold, or are you just trying to encourage me?'

'Yes, I do,' said the giant without a moment's hesitation.

Above them a kingly eagle hovered, riding the thermals of the air on outstretched wings: soaring, spiralling, diving, moving with incredible speed and power, surfing on the wild waves of the wind. Seldom had such grace and majesty been seen in the deadlands of Dimrat. Higher than the reach of human sight he flew, gazing downward telescopically. Hooded eyes that had watched the birth of stars and planets, followed the giant and the girl caringly. In the midst of Dimrat's desolation, they were not alone.

The eagle cried out, a wild, majestic shriek that carried across the oceans of the sky.

A great feeling of peace and courage seized Joanna. 'That's strange,' she said. 'I feel different somehow. Do you?'

'Not really. I only have this feeling that I'm in the right place, that this is where I should be.'

'I felt a shadow lift from my mind. Maybe I was just imagining it. This place does weird things to you.' Joanna was silent for a few seconds. 'It was . . .' she paused, her face twisted in a frown and her eyes unfocused. 'It was a comforting feeling like . . .' She shrugged her shoulders. 'I can't explain it, but it was almost as if a voice said: "You're going to be okay; everything will work out. Don't be afraid."'

The house was close; the door loomed before them, a grimy rectangle of wood held by rusty hinges.

Rumbold approached it and studied it carefully, probing the wood with his fingertips, searching for a weakness in its construction.

'Can we get in?' enquired Joanna anxiously.

'Easily!' replied Rumbold. 'Dimrat doesn't expect visitors, so he's not particular about security.'

Rumbold stood before the door, balancing on his toes with his back slightly arched—a fighter's pose. Almost too quickly for Joanna to see, the giant kicked the door. His booted foot crashed into the woodwork inches below the lock and the door splintered and fell inwards. The way into the House of Many Rooms was open.

'Which way shall we go?' she asked uncertainly.

'Follow the drift of the smog. That should lead us to our destination.'

The house was full of sounds: hissing, squeaking, growling, screaming, gnashing and the scampering and shuffling of feet. Each closed door, each twist of passageway and staircase held the threat of danger. Rumbold drew his sword from its scabbard and walked behind Joanna, his eyes vigilant.

The smog drifted from the grumbling belly of the house, rising, always rising, drifting upwards in tattered wisps. Rumbold and Joanna tracked it. Passage followed passage, stairway followed stairway, until they came to the lowest level of the House of Many Rooms: a cavern lit by the spiteful glow of electric light bulbs. In the far wall was a door, and from it billowed the smog that was poisoning the world.

'It's there,' whispered Rumbold, pointing in the direction of the patch of darkness. 'That's the door. We've made it. Now to get the key.' But before they could approach it, two shapes exploded from the opening and sped towards them howling: grey fur bristling with fury, mad eyes ablaze, fangs bloodied and murderous.

149

'Kilvarsts! Giant kilvarsts!' screamed Joanna, but before she could say more, Rumbold had leapt in front of her, his sword in his hand. In a second the kilvarsts were upon them, one behind the other, leaping at Rumbold, hurling themselves upon him: mad, tormented minds intent on his destruction. As the first of them arched through the air, Rumbold impaled it in mid-leap, the sword blade tearing the creature's head apart, spattering its mate with blood and splintered bone. But even the impact of the blow could not stop its charge. A twitching corpse, it fell upon Rumbold, dangerous even in death. The collision threw Rumbold from his feet, and before he could recover, the second kilvarst was upon him, jaws wide and frothing, snapping, snarling, tearing at the giant's throat. Its claws buried in the muscles of his back. Rumbold seized the kilvarst's head and held it from him.

Seeing the danger, Joanna grabbed Rumbold's fallen sword and dashed to him. 'Hold its head still!' she screamed. 'Hold it still!' Pinning the creature's writhing body in a wrestler's leg lock, Rumbold gripped its head in both his hands and held it motionless. Joanna drove the blade downwards with all her strength, shattering the transparent dome that protected its brain and killing the creature instantly.

Rumbold climbed unsteadily to his feet. 'You're hurt. There's blood on your shoulder and back,' said Joanna, her voice expressing the concern that shone in her eyes.

'Nothing much. Only a scratch or two,' he replied. 'Thanks! Thanks for helping me.' His voice was warm and sincere.

A cruel, angry shriek shook Rumbold and Joanna to tingling alertness. 'It's the masquith,' gasped Rumbold. 'Dimrat must have returned. Go! You'll have to find the key alone. I'll hold off Dimrat and the masquith for as long as possible; long enough to give you a chance to find the key. Go now!'

'But you don't have any weapons.'

'I've got my sword. That's all I need.'

'Your sword?' said Joanna scornfully. 'What use is a sword against Dimrat and his masquith? Come with me, Rumbold. Come with me.' She reached out to him, her eyes pleading, but he stood firm.

'No, I cannot come.' He looked at her, wanting to say the things that he had hidden from her. Instead, he clumsily took her in his arms and held her like a child. 'Goodbye. Goodbye, Joanna,' he whispered, and then he broke free from her and raced to meet the killer of his people.

Joanna was alone.

24

The Sword of Rumbold

Down streaked the masquith, her cruel talons clawing the sky before her. She saw the shattered door and shrieked in fury. Down, down she sped, each beat of her monstrous wings a thunderclap. She was the most terrible of Dimrat's creatures, a pterodactyl from earth's distant past, but larger, fiercer, more cunning and deadly. During the years of exile, Dimrat had created her from the frozen body of her long dead mother. No warm blood flowed in her veins and arteries; no crimson dragonfire blazed in her jaws, only the terrible cold of the ice-lands that had nurtured her. Down she swooped, her freezing breath turning the clouds about her to hail and blizzards of driving snow. Grey hoar-frost clung to her leathery wings and icicles hung from her belly like fields of glittering swords; her eyes crackled with fury.

Saddled between the shoulders of the masquith, Dimrat saw the shattered door and understood her rage. 'I've been tricked,' he screamed, his voice only a whisper above the hurricane beat of her wings. 'Curse that girl! Curse the Maker! Faster! Faster!' He beat the masquith's shoulders with his hands, a pathetic, futile gesture. 'Faster!' The masquith needed no encouragement. She shot through the sky, wings stretched back, head thrust forward and talons curled beneath her, a raging gale of evil power. 'I've been tricked, outwitted by a stupid girl. I'll kill you!' he snarled. 'I'll kill you!'

Beneath them, a figure sprang through the ruined door and waited. 'Rumbold! You fool!' cried Dimrat, recognising him. 'Do you think you can stand in my way, in the way of the one who made you?' But his words were lost in the shriek of the masquith. With a violent jolt that almost shook Dimrat from his perch between her shoulders, she landed.

Rumbold stood before the door, his sword unsheathed and the stalking fog closing in about him. He saw each sequence of his life as if he were a spectator looking on. Everything became dazzlingly clear. He remembered his fugitive years, hunted by the nazdargs and their masters; his meeting with Joanna; their journey to the House of Many Rooms. 'All the roads I've trodden,' he whispered, in a sudden burst of insight, 'meet at this broken door.'

'Move out of my way,' commanded Dimrat. 'Don't you recognise me, Gendast?' He used Rumbold's former name. 'I'm your maker. What's the point in pretending you're anything different? Move or you will not live to see another grey dawn.' The masquith watched Rumbold with eyes as pitiless as ice, her body tensed to spring.

Rumbold's voice was calm and steady. 'I'm not of you, Dimrat. I'm the Captain's. He's my master.'

'You're mad! I'm your maker, and your precious Captain's not around to help you. Not that he intended to help. He's deceived you. He's afraid to meet me himself so he's manipulated you.'

The giant laughed sadly. 'You don't change, Dimrat; always twisting the noble things of life with your lies and treachery. The Captain, afraid of you? What ruler ever cleanses his kingdom of vermin? He uses his servants to do it!'

'Enough! You've said enough. The hour of your death has come!' The masquith's fury robbed her of her cunning. She charged the giant, lurching towards him clumsily. Rumbold leapt aside, easily avoiding her. He swivelled on his toes and ran in beneath the shadow of a wing. The great sword sang, once, twice, cutting through the masquith's frozen skin, finding the vulnerable organs beneath. She screamed and fell on Rumbold, attempting to crush him beneath her massive bulk, but he was too quick for her. He leapt aside, turned, and sprang in again, dodging her talons and cruel, searching beak with lightning reflexes. The sword slashed downwards, slicing the corded muscle and severing the wing. With a wild shriek of agony, the masquith retreated into the fog.

'Take your crippled bird and fly away!' shouted Rumbold, his voice muffled by the fog. Dimrat and the masquith had vanished.

Pain had turned the masquith's rage into a cold, determined fighting fury. Her eyes watched Rumbold through the fog, studying him, waiting with the hunter's instinct for the right moment to attack. Dimrat sensed the mood of his creature; felt the tension and suspense in the coiled muscles of her back and came to her assistance.

'Gendast!' he called, in a low, scornful voice. 'I enjoyed the murder of your brethren. Such precious moments. Do you remember? Of course you do! You were there, watching all the time. Smell the burning flesh of your mother; see her writhing; hear her screams. Ah, what music! And what about your sisters? What about them? The boiling oil we poured into their ears; our clapping and laughter as they screamed. You do remember, don't you?' He paused and searched the fog with his eyes. He heard a stifled cry and laughed. 'You do remember. That's good. That's very good. What would life be like without some happy memories, Gendast?'

Agony clouded Rumbold's eyes and his hands trembled with the terror of the memory. Seizing her chance, the masquith leapt at Rumbold, bursting through the fog upon him.

Pain! Unendurable pain! Rumbold's sword whined in fury. A turn of his wrists, a sudden lunge, and the blade tore out the eye of the shrieking masquith, shattering her beak and bone. Crippled and beaten, she fled again into the fog. Rumbold stood unbroken before the door.

'Dimrat,' he shouted, 'I give you one last chance. Return to the ice-lands of your exile. Leave this land for ever!'

'How can I?' countered Dimrat. 'You've crippled my bird.' And then he laughed. 'Move from the door!' The masquith dragged herself towards Rumbold through the fog: a monstrous, shadowy beast, lame but dangerous. 'Move, I tell you!' commanded Dimrat, but before Rumbold could reply, he gave a shrill whistle.

'Go!' cried the giant, but Dimrat only laughed. Reverently, Rumbold raised his sword above his head. The movement drew from the blade a low, sweet note. His spirit animated the weapon, turning the dull blade incandescent. With a sudden twist of his wrists, Rumbold wielded the sword in a wide arc above him; the blade sang with triumph, its sharp edges burned with fire. The sword leapt and danced in the giant's hand, each complicated manoeuvre eliciting its own special note from the singing blade. Rumbold joined his voice to the music of the sword and sang a battle chant. In the grey land of Dimrat, the sword wove patterns of coloured light, driving back the fog with its brilliance.

As Rumbold's voice reached its crescendo, a terrible sound was heard from the House of Many Rooms. A babble of cries, screams, howls, roars, inhuman voices, rushing feet and beating wings approached. At first the sound was faint, but it grew rapidly in power until the giant's song was silenced. All the windows of the house were shattered simultaneously, bursting outwards in a hail of splintered glass and speeding bodies. Hosts of red-eyed bats, wolves and rabid hunting dogs, rats and giant spiders, snakes and flying scorpions, along with tiny biting, stinging creatures formed in Dimrat's laboratories— all rushed upon Rumbold. Before the attack overwhelmed him, he gave a great, despairing cry.

Dimrat laughed and watched the fight with cruel pleasure. 'How do you like my pets, Gendast?' he enquired mockingly. 'I've always been an animal lover! I just can't get enough fresh meat. It's such a shame. But thanks for feeding them.' He laughed at his own insane humour.

The creatures clawed, bit and stung, covering Rumbold's body like maggots on the carcass of a sheep. He fell and rose again, his sword hacking at his attackers without respite. Its killing song was terrible: a song of blood and savage triumph. A battle rage sustained the giant long after his natural strength had fled. The tiny part of his consciousness that was still self-aware told him he was dying, but life and death meant nothing to him.

When it was over and the last of the creatures lay broken and twitching at his feet, Rumbold staggered, falling down on one knee, the land reeling and turning to darkness before him. The cold, mocking laughter of Dimrat bit into his ears.

'You've killed my poor little pets. How cruel of you!'

He felt tired, more tired than he had ever been in his life. With an enormous effort of will, he stood upright and forced his eyes to focus. His vision became clearer. Dimrat straddled the masquith before him, his evil lips twisted in laughter. A great sadness overcame him. 'I've failed the Captain, failed Joanna,' he thought. He tried to hold their faces in his memory, but they were being sucked from him into a dark, forgetful place.

Dimrat read his anguish. 'You've failed, Gendast,' he mocked. 'The girl's mine, mine to play with and abuse. I think I'll take her to my laboratories and make something of her.'

In Rumbold's hour of distress, bleeding with many bitter wounds, there came and stood by him the once wounded Captain. He looked upon the giant with great love and held him tenderly in his arms as a mother does a fretful child.

'It's you!' whispered the giant in a weak and broken voice. 'You've come! I knew you would!'

'Well done, old friend. The sword I gave you has been used well, but the battle's not over. It's not your destiny to die in sorrow, your task unfinished.' With these words, the Captain breathed upon the giant and vanished from his sight, leaving him standing before the shattered door surrounded by the corpses of his enemies.

Like a dream in which hours, days and weeks are squeezed into a moment, the Captain's coming and words to Rumbold were over in a second. Dimrat and his masquith saw only a sudden smile of joy and recognition flicker in the giant's eyes and then die out. With his life spilling out from countless wounds,

Rumbold stood and waited. His bloodied sword tip rested in the ground between his feet.

Certain of Rumbold's defeat, the masquith charged again, her freezing breath stinging his bleeding wounds.

Rumbold crouched, the huge slabs of muscle on his ruined body tensed for the spring. The Captain's breath had strengthened him. As the masquith fell upon him, Rumbold exploded upwards, unleashing all the power of his body in the sword thrust. The blade sparkled, igniting in a blaze of white hot fire. Piercing the folds of calloused skin, it shattered the great arched bones of the masquith's ribcage and ripped its heart apart. The masquith screamed in pain and outrage, her one good wing beating the air in a futile attempt to escape from the burning agony of the blade. Rumbold withdrew the sword and leapt aside, cold blood spurting across his body. The masquith stiffened, wobbled on her legs and slowly tumbled over. *Crash!* Muscles twitched and jerked and then grew still.

It was only then that Dimrat realised his danger. 'Gendast,' he wheedled, 'I'm sure we can come to some agreement.' His voice was a desperate, pleading whine. 'I'm your true father, Gendast. You can't deny that. I made you. Gendast, would you kill your father?'

Rumbold was silent, his torn and wounded body rising out of the fog before Dimrat; his eyes as unforgiving and relentless as an executioner's and his sword murmuring angrily in his hands, its edges scorched with crimson fire. Death towered over Dimrat.

He saw at last his danger. With a stifled howl of terror, Dimrat leapt from the carcass of the masquith and raced towards the shelter of the fog. Rumbold heaved back his sword and cast it at the retreating figure, the blade leaping from his hands and spinning through the air like a wheel of shrieking fire. The momentum of the throw hurled the blade through Dimrat's back and chest and out of the other side. Skewered, Dimrat staggered on for a few paces and then collapsed upon his face. The sword tip spiked the ground beneath him, impaling him to the grey earth.

Only seconds before, the land had been stable. Now it shook and trembled. A huge chasm opened at Rumbold's feet and swallowed Dimrat, the sword still spiking him. An earthquake shook the island. The lake foamed and roared. Great geysers erupted from it and shot skywards; furious waves attacked the shoreline, frothing white in the madness of their rage and torment.

Above the roar of the earthquake, Rumbold heard a sharp explosion. He turned and saw jagged cracks appearing in the walls of the House of Many Rooms. The entire building was collapsing. Summoning the last of his strength, he threw himself through the door and began the descent into the cavern. With a roar like an avalanche, the roof above him slowly sagged and fell inwards. 'Joanna! Joanna!' he cried in desperation. 'I'm coming!'

25

The Legions of the Dead

The kilvarsts lay dead at her feet. In the distance she could hear the screams of battle. Joanna's immediate instinct was to run to the side of Rumbold and stand by him in his fight with Dimrat, but she knew that any help that she could offer would be futile; her duty lay elsewhere.

The door stood open like a hungry mouth, and from its jaws poured the dreadful darkness that had driven the song and colour from the land. Joanna's fear was swept away by a sudden surge of anger. She thought of the sad-faced people, the children with frightened eyes and lips that never smiled, the forests of crippled trees, the songless birds and withered, dying flowers. All the remorse and sadness of the land came upon her in that moment. She seemed to rise above the evil halls of Dimrat and see the land stretched out before her: the grey sea breaking on grey sand; the grey rivers and grey mountains towering into the vaster greyness of the sky; the grey fields and hedgerows; the grey hamlets and towns; the grey, despairing people. To the north, east, south and west, the land was desolate and colourless.

Her anger gave her courage. She leapt through the door and came to a sudden stop, an involuntary squeal of amazement whistling from her lips. She was in a crowded shopping mall. A fierce artificial light beat against her eyes, and the crowd roared in torrents about her like a river in flood. There were no shop assistants or security guards and all the goods were free. 'It's just like Oxford Street on the first day of the January sales,' she thought.

A lean man with a mean, pinched face slammed into her in his haste to reach a nearby jeweller's, knocking her to one side. 'You could say sorry,' she protested angrily, but he ignored her. Joanna followed him and watched as he crammed necklaces, brooches and other trinkets into his pockets. 'Where is this place?' she demanded, but the man ignored her. 'I'm talking to you,' she persisted, and her eyes cut into him, sharp as lasers.

The man began to push rings onto his spidery fingers, cursing under his breath if one did not fit.

'We're the dead,' he snarled, not bothering to look up. 'This is the country of the dead. Now get lost!'

Joanna staggered from the shop and looked about her in horror. The people were shameless in their greed, rushing from one shop to another, in a fever of desire, their flesh glistening like hot wax.

An escalator carried a long stream of shoppers into the lower levels of the mall, and drifting upwards against the flow of bodies rose the grey smog. Joanna struggled towards the escalator, and behind her a figure followed, his dark features hidden in the shadow of a cowl. As she descended, the light grew steadily weaker: a dull, sickly glow that leaked from the walls about her, making the nightmare landscape visible. The shop displays in the lower levels of the mall had turned to powdery dust or had decayed beyond recognition.

Joanna could see great hosts of shadow people rising to meet her. 'Daughter! Daughter! Have mercy upon us!' they cried, their voices rustling like dry leaves in a sudden squall of wind. Joanna wept at the sight of them, her revulsion overcome by pity. Peace eluded them. Unable to remain still, not even for a moment, they shuffled restlessly about, their thin, reed-like voices rising in murmurs of grief. 'You are of the living,' they cried and stared at her with a terrible hunger.

The things that had enslaved the people on earth continued to enslave them in the underworld. Kings, whose word had ruled empires, were chained to vast hoards of treasure. Merchants, whose ships had navigated the treacherous highways of the sea, were chained to chests of gold coins, jewels and rare spices. Warlords, whose swords had gorged on innocent blood, were chained to dragons who devoured whole armies but were never satisfied. Lovers, whose lust had been their life's obsession, were chained to

160

monsters, demons, lizards and all manner of repulsive reptiles. Vain women, whose beauty had seduced the world, were chained to mirrors of polished glass.

The mall was a desert of dust and neglect. The great deserts of Joanna's world were lush gardens by comparison. This was the great desert, the awful original, from which all other deserts were named. Here no raindrop splashed on parched stone, no sunlight filtered through a fissure in the rock, no flowers grew, and no seasons changed the monotony of the dead land. Nothing lived except the memory of life lost.

Down, down, down she travelled, passing through the countries of the dead, the cowled figure sticking to her like a shadow. As she approached the centre of the kingdom, the glare grew brighter, a cold, hateful light without warmth or comfort. Joanna shivered and felt her vulnerability: a tiny speck of life surrounded by encroaching desert.

The hall was so immense that Joanna could not see the distant walls. Before her in the chamber stood a desk, and behind it in a huge executive chair sat the pale figure of the manageress, the ruler of the dead. Tall she sat, and terrible, clutching her sickle with which she harvested the souls of men. Her yellow eyes stalked Joanna with a cold, pitiless malice.

'Come here, child,' she commanded. Her voice was horrible, a dry rasping whisper that filled the world.

'Help me! Help me!' whispered Joanna as she felt the last remnants of her courage slip away. 'If only this were a dream,' she thought, 'I'd wake up and it'd be over.' The cowled figure touched her and gave her back her voice. 'I've come for the key,' she said.

'The key?' echoed the pale manageress. 'What key?'

'The key to the door of the underworld,' she replied.

'Oh! The one key; the great key; the only key. You want that key, girl?'

'Yes please,' said Joanna weakly.

The manageress threw her head back and laughed, the echoes repeating the sound until it seemed as if the entire underworld was laughing at Joanna. 'Being polite, are we?' she said. 'I've always been partial to good manners. I know what we'll do. We'll play a little game for the key, just you and me. What do you say?'

Because she could think of no better way to obtain it, Joanna agreed. 'I'll play if I know the game,' she said.

'You'll pick it up very quickly, my dear,' intoned the manageress in a voice intended to be reassuring. 'There's really nothing to it, nothing to it at all!' The manageress seemed highly amused and beamed at Joanna in a fair imitation of good humour. 'The odds are even,' she said. 'Now I wouldn't think of cheating you, would I dear child?'

'I'm sure you wouldn't,' said Joanna sincerely. Things were turning out better than she had imagined.

'Come here! Sit on this stool, girl!' commanded the manageress.

Joanna obeyed. 'It can become very boring in this world. Nobody here likes playing games. They're a tiresome crowd. All they do is flit around and talk about the past. They've got no life!' she confided. The manageress opened a drawer in her desk and presented Joanna with a box of engraved marble. 'This is the game. Would you like to open it?' she enquired.

'Oh! Yes please. Are you sure you don't mind?'

'No, it's a pleasure, a real pleasure.' Joanna opened the box and gasped.

'It's a gun,' she cried. 'What sort of game is this?'

'In your world,' answered the manageress, 'it's called Russian Roulette!'

26

Russian Roulette

Joanna's protests were futile. 'It's not fair!' she cried. 'I won't play.' But the manageress silenced her with eyes as hard as tombstones.

'You promised to play,' whispered the manageress, her voice cold and soft like snow. 'Until you agree to play the game, your promise will bind you in my kingdom for ever. The prize is the key.' With these words, she slipped the key from around her neck and cast it on the desk, its sharp clatter ringing out like a challenge, summoning the hosts of the dead to the contest.

The terror that Joanna felt was so utter and complete that she was paralysed. Around her were the legions of the dead, a restless sea of hollow faces, withered limbs and ravenous, tormented eyes. The manageress interpreted Joanna's silence as agreement. 'Me first. I'll show you how to play it.' She took the gun, lifted it to her head and pulled the trigger. *Bang!* The gun detonated but she was unharmed. Without taking her eyes from Joanna's face, she spun the cylinder and handed the gun to the trembling girl. 'A blank shell,' she explained. 'Just a little joke of mine. It's a game after all.' And her lips curled upwards in a slow snarl of a smile.

Joanna's hand was unsteady. She felt the barrel of the revolver jerking against the side of her head. The cylinder was still warm from use and smoke bled from the barrel. She squeezed her eyes tightly shut and pulled the trigger in the same moment. The hammer seemed to descend in slow motion, an instant stretched into a lifetime. In her imagination, she was old and crippled, her skin hanging from her face in untidy folds. A wheelchair defined the frontiers of her world. The manageress appeared. 'Come!' she commanded. Too tired and weak to resist, Joanna followed, her life slipping away in a long, regretful sigh.

Click! The hammer of the gun found an empty cylinder. The evil dream fell from Joanna. She was alive. Alive and young again!

Each time Joanna pulled the trigger she hallucinated. Click! She was a soldier riddled with bullets on a battlefield far from home. Click! She was a leper with a mutilated body covered in festering sores. Click! She was a cancer patient in an intensive care unit pleading for morphine. Click! She was a tiny child with a distended belly, starving in her mother's arms. Click! She was a road accident victim lying in a pool of blood. Click! Click! Click! The manageress of death stalked her in a thousand different disguises.

Joanna reached out again and took the revolver from the manageress' hand.

'Can't we stop—please?' she pleaded, but the manageress only laughed.

'Get on with it, child. Get it over with. It can't be long now.' Her eyes were boiling pits of evil in the pale horror of her face. 'Did you think that you could really challenge me, child? Did you think that I'd give up my key so easily? Have you no idea of the greatness of my power?' As she spoke, the manageress grew tall and terrible. 'I am the mistress of the world, of all worlds. All those who live must come to me. Have you no sense or understanding, child? Look at my subjects,' she cried, and she pointed at the countless armies of the dead. 'Egypt! Assyria! Babylon! Greece! Rome! Your own country! They're all here—all my subjects! Did you think that you could win my key— a mere child? Now get on with it. Take the gun: pull the trigger. Die!'

Despair! Joanna lifted the gun and pointed it at her

temple. It was heavy and awkward in her hand. She curled her finger round the trigger and began to pull, but before she could complete the movement, the cowled figure became visible. He rose before Joanna, huge, all powerful, his upper body penetrating the cavern roof. Rock was no obstacle to him: the underworld had no power over him at all. Casting aside his cowl and cloak, he stood before Joanna in terrible majesty, garlanded with stars and robed in crackling lightning. In his eyes she saw the universe reflected. All the boundless distances of space were there: vast meadows sown with flowers of glittering light, captured in the glory of his gaze. From the fall of a snowflake to the supernova of a giant sun, nothing escaped him. He was the Captain, the Maker of the worlds.

Joanna fell on her knees before him, her young body trembling with a tender, holy fear and her face bright with wonder. 'It's you! It's really you! You've come,' said Joanna in a tiny, timid voice.

'I've been with you all the time, but you could not see me. Even now I'm invisible to the manageress. You didn't really think I'd let you face her all alone, did you?'

'I thought you might try to help, but I didn't know if you could. I don't know enough about you.'

The Maker spoke with a chuckle in his voice. 'Well, we'll have to do something about that, won't we?' he said. 'And there's also this little question of Russian Roulette. The manageress played it with me, you know, some years ago. She never recovered. She tries to forget, but that won't change anything. She's a fake. Dangerous? Certainly! Powerful? Of course! But a fake all the same. There's something she didn't tell you, Joanna. Look!' The Captain opened his hand, and in the palm was a single bullet. 'The revolver's empty,' he said quietly. 'I've got the only bullet.' With those words he reached out and touched Joanna's lips with his fingertips. 'Sing!' he commanded.

Her eyes were opened and she saw the Captain's country, only for a moment, but it was enough. Sweet, clean air fizzed in her lungs and the colours were more brilliant than any she had ever seen in her life. Music lilted all about her: the wind crooning in the trees and long grass; the rivers singing in a deep bass as they strolled the valleys, or in a high soprano as they raced down hills and mountain slopes; birds singing in the chorus or pausing to listen to a solo performance. It was a magical trilling of notes that seemed to stun the world to silence.

'Get up and pull yourself together. Get on with it, child. What are you waiting for?' rasped the manageress impatiently, unaware of the presence of the Captain and jerking on Joanna's elbow. 'What are you doing grovelling on the floor?'

Joanna laughed, a joyful, pure sound, and began to sing; the Spirit of the Captain gave her words and melody:

> Night is over;
> Shadows vanish.
> Sun is rising;
> Day is dawning.
> Death is conquered;
> Fear is vanquished.
> Dimrat's power
> At last is broken.
>
> Colours tumble
> From the morning;
> Wind is blowing;
> Darkness fleeing.
> Death is conquered;
> Fear is vanquished.
> Dimrat's power
> At last is broken.
>
> Watch! the land is
> Slowly waking.

Children laughing;
Voices singing.
Death is conquered;
Fear is vanquished.
Dimrat's power
At last is broken.

Death is slain;
The keys are taken.
Trees are budding;
Flowers dancing.
Death is conquered;
Fear is vanquished.
Dimrat's power
At last is broken.

'Stop!' screeched the manageress. She was no longer a tall, terrifying figure, but a withered crone hiding in the corner of a seat grown suddenly too large for her. 'Stop! I can't stand it!' she squealed.

Joanna threw down the revolver and sang with greater joy and power, the notes trembling in the stillness, ricocheting from the walls, swelling, multiplying, until it seemed as if her one voice had become a mighty choir. At the sound of her song, the foundations of the underworld shook and trembled and the rocks groaned in pain. The curse was broken. Huge cracks appeared in the floor at her feet and rushed outwards like giant tendrils. Rocks broke from the roof of the chamber and fell around her. But still she sang as the underworld crashed in about her.

At last the song ended. Seizing the key, she fled along the passage that led to her world. She ran as she had never run before: racing the white hot lava that followed at her heels; dodging the rocks that crashed and splintered around her; hurling herself through endless curtains of coarse, clinging dust; driving herself onwards, upwards, the stench of sulphur scorching her lungs and stinging her eyes.

She ran until she thought her body would explode with the effort.

The door was before her, a tiny rectangle of pale light. With one last desperate spurt, she reached it, leapt through it, slammed it shut, and, resting her shoulder upon its heaving surface, drove the key into the keyhole and turned it.

27

From the Garden to the Stars

A chill, night breeze drove away the grey and the moon appeared, a pool of gold reeking of mystery. Stars jewelled the night and the colours crept back to the land, their brilliance subdued by darkness. But the mire of Filcheeth clung to her clothes and limbs and the grey remained in the girl's soul, an opaque cloud that blinded her to the miracle that was taking place about her. Joanna shivered and remembered, her eyes bright with tears.

'Rumbold!' she whispered, and his name shattered her heart and left her with a numbing emptiness. Hours had passed, stretching out behind her like a lifetime. She sat alone with her grief, the stones and timbers of Dimrat's ruined house piled high around her.

Joanna remembered cowering before the closed door, the manageress' key imbedded in the lock, forbidding the grey smog. Masonry tumbled around her and a beam had pinned her to the wall. She remembered the quick beat of running feet and Rumbold leaping into the basement and hauling the beam from her. She had screamed at the sight of his ravaged body. His flesh was shredded and his features had been torn from his face.

'Run!' he commanded. 'Run, Joanna!'

'What's Dimrat done to you?' she cried, her voice raw with anguish. But before Rumbold could reply, the ceiling sagged and fell inwards with a roar. Rumbold threw himself beneath a girder and used his body as a wedge. The ceiling groaned and heaved, but Rumbold held it from collapse.

'Run!' he implored, and his eyes smote her like a commandment. Joanna ran, her heart ruptured and her eyes weeping blood. She had wanted to stay with Rumbold, share her friend's last moments, but she was unable to disobey him. Even as she ran and sobbed, she felt the truth within her: he had given his life for her, the best gift any friend could give to another, and she could not scorn it.

Joanna wept and raged as the House of Many Rooms collapsed: wept for Rumbold crushed in the ruin of the house, and raged at her own impotence.

'Captain! You could have done something,' she shouted, her voice drowned in the thunder of falling masonry. 'Where are you? Where are you?' She recalled the Captain's face so vividly that the accusation petered on her lips. 'It doesn't make sense,' she groaned and her eyes flooded with tears.

She had found Rumbold after a long search. His body was concealed by boulders and only his face was visible, his eyes as blank as the windows of an empty house. 'He's gone,' she muttered, deranged by grief and shock. 'This broken thing is not Rumbold.' She raised her voice: 'Rumbold! Rumbold! Where are you?' But there was no answer, only the hungry buzz of a fly scavenging for flesh. She brushed it from Rumbold's face and then tried to move the boulders that covered him, but her efforts were futile. He ended his life where he began it: a prisoner in Dimrat's House of Many Rooms.

And so the night passed, the beginning of many nights: stars winged like angels in silvery light and the radiant moon draped in borrowed gold. But the girl did not notice. Alone in her grief, she saw only the grey.

Dawn came slowly and doused the embers of the stars with floods of light. Joanna kept watch beside Rumbold, the early sun casting her shadow across his face in mourning.

'Joanna!' The voice was deep and familiar.

Joanna turned round, her eyes screwed up against the blaze of the sun. 'It's you,' she exclaimed in a flat voice. 'You've come too late. He's dead.' And she turned from the Captain, her shoulders squared in rejection.

The Captain's boots were caked in mud and he was dressed as a gardener: khaki trousers, an open-necked shirt and a red necktie. He clambered over the debris of the house, sat down next to Joanna and placed his arm about her shoulders. She tensed but did not draw away. They sat silently together, gazing down at Rumbold.

'I loved him too, you know,' said the Captain, breaking the silence.

Joanna looked at him and saw tears glistening in his eyes. 'But why didn't you help him like you helped me? He didn't deserve to die.'

The Captain was silent, but his face became transparent as it had done on the airship. Joanna saw all the suffering and injustices of life reflected in it, a sudden kaleidoscope of images: the world's pain poured into his soul. He made no attempt to answer her question, but she glimpsed his agony and felt the fierce heat of his love.

'He cares. He really cares!' she thought. Joanna had known this from the beginning, but now she was certain of it. She leaped the rift of doubt that lay between them and clung to the Captain. 'I trust you! I trust you before all others. You are the Captain, the Maker of the worlds,' she confessed, and the grey was banished from her spirit.

The Captain's hands were rough and calloused, bruised by work and creation. He placed them gently about the giant's ruined face and leaned towards him. 'Wake up, old friend,' he whispered. 'Morning has come and the colours have returned to the land.' Joanna gave a startled, joyful cry. The giant's disfigured face became whole, the grey granite of his skin changed to a rich purple, and his eyes opened, the irises brown-flecked with dancing motes of gold.

Rumbold smiled at the Captain, his gentle, crooked smile. 'Is this your country?' he asked, and Joanna thrilled to the sound of his voice.

'No! This is your land and the colours have returned.'

'Colour!' Rumbold cried and attempted to sit up, but the weight of the boulders held him back. Suddenly he remembered and a shadow passed across his face: 'Joanna . . . is she safe? Is she alive?'

'Yes!' she answered and came forward and knelt over him, her fingers caressing his cheek.

Rumbold turned to the Captain. 'We won. We've defeated Dimrat. The land is free again.' And he hurled the boulders from his body and leaped upright, smooth, hard flesh and corded muscle visible through his ragged battle dress.

Rumbold towered over Joanna. 'Thanks for saving me,' she said and looked up at him shyly. The tough image had cracked wide open, and she stood before him, a tall, lovely girl in the bloom of early womanhood. Words were an intrusion, so they gazed at each other in silence. 'There are some friends,' thought Joanna, 'who are dearer than a lover.'

'Come! There's work to do,' commanded the

Captain. 'Here, take these,' he said and offered them two baskets filled with seeds. Some Joanna recognised, like the common acorn, but many were unknown.

'What do we do with them?' she enquired, confusion showing clearly on her face.

'You scatter them!' The Captain plucked a handful of seeds from Joanna's basket and clambered from the ruins of the House of Many Rooms. 'Watch!' He threw the seeds onto the blackened soil and they vanished, burrowing into the earth like insects. 'Now watch!' he said, and his voice held them in its power. Suddenly the earth around the Captain erupted. Saplings sprang from the soil and grew with astonishing speed: alder, walnut and a giant oak, branches clothed in every shade of green. The Captain smiled at their amazement. 'It is your task to replant the forest, but leave a broad stretch of land from the eastern edge of the island to Dimrat's ruined house. I'm going to plant a garden. Go!'

'I wish my mother were here to share this,' said Rumbold. 'She loved all living things.'

'Your mother?' exclaimed Joanna in surprise. 'I thought you were created in the motherlobes.'

'No. They were introduced after Dimrat's failure to control the giants. He forced women to co-operate with his genetic experiments, using them as surrogate mothers. I was lucky. My mother didn't reject me. Her love and teaching turned me from the ways of Dimrat. She was killed in the massacre, but a little bit of her still lives inside me. If I close my eyes and listen, I can still hear her voice: "The world is beautiful, Rumbold, a floating garden in the sea of space. Care for it and the colours will return." She taught me to reverence life.'

Rumbold and Joanna laboured and a new forest arose, a ring of green that circled the island like a crown. The air was sweet with the smell of cedars, larch and cypress, and the leaves wove a canopy above the girl and the giant, shading them from the sun. White anemones frosted the forest floor, and orchids, violets and yellow archangels grew between the trees in limpid pools of light. The forest awoke and sang: aspen and elm, spruce and whitebeam, joining their voices in harmony. In the midst of their celebrations, the birds returned in flocks and sang with them, a pure, joyful sound that trilled among the trees as if that day were the beginning of the world.

It was evening when Joanna and Rumbold cast their last seeds into the soil and stumbled back to the House of Many Rooms, their shadows trailing them. Lawns and gardens greeted them and Dimrat's ruined house had been turned into a rockery.

The Captain was waiting. 'Come! Let me show you what I've done.' They followed him along a narrow path that meandered through the rockery, marvelling at the flowers and shrubs that grew there. 'See! I've made a lake,' said the Captain. The debris had vanished, and in its place was a ring of clear water, rimmed by willows and fed by a spring. He opened his hands and tiny, silver fish appeared and wriggled between his fingers into the water with a pitter-patter like rain. 'Our work is finished. It's time to eat, but before we do, you'd better wash and change, Joanna. Your clothes are covered in mud.'

'I've lost my backpack and don't have a change of clothes,' replied Joanna apologetically. 'The mud is from the fens of Filcheeth.'

The Captain smiled and added: 'I always seem to be returning your lost property,' and he lifted Joanna's backpack from behind an ornamental shrub. 'Here!' he said, tossing the backpack to Joanna. 'I found it in the ruins of Dimrat's house. Make yourself respectable.'

Joanna had picked wild strawberries and plums in the forest, but she had eaten little that day. She washed and changed quickly, ogled her reflection in the mirror-smooth lake, and then joined the Captain and Rumbold for dinner. The Captain had prepared a feast of wild duck and fruit. He blessed the food and invited them to eat. As they feasted, the sun tripped over the world's edge and splashed the sky with stars.

Joanna sat close to Rumbold and dreamed a secret, joyful dream of a lifetime in which they would never part—friends for ever! When the meal was finished, a deep hush fell upon the company, and the island and the sky above it were bathed in mysterious light. 'It's time for us to leave you, Joanna,' said the Captain, and he stood up.

'Leave me?' cried Joanna in alarm. 'Where are you going?' Her heart cracked in two and her dreams were broken in a moment.

'Home! Rumbold is coming with me.'

'But he belongs here; here in this land,' protested Joanna, and clutched the giant's hand.

Rumbold tenderly unloosed her fingers. 'He tells the truth, Joanna. I died and this is the body of my resurrection. I do not belong here. I belong in the Captain's country,' He knelt before her and took her hands in his. 'Goodbye, my sister.' He brushed her forehead with his lips.

The sky opened and Joanna glimpsed the Captain's country. A bridge spanned both worlds and the Captain took the giant's hand and led him across.

Joanna wept, not for Rumbold but for herself. She saw the gates of the sky close behind them and knew that she would never see the giant again.

The moon was full and the lawns were carpeted in gold. Joanna sat with her back against the trunk of a magnolia tree and listened to the tinkle of the spring and the murmur of the wind in the treetops. She sat alone like a forsaken bride, the white blossom of the magnolia tree clinging to her hair and clothes like confetti. At last, worn out by the labours of the day and the pain of losing Rumbold, she sank into an exhausted sleep.

Joanna was awakened in the morning by the thunder of whirling blades. A gunship flew in low over the forest and dipped towards her. She was about to run for the cover of the trees when a familiar voice boomed down at her: 'Don't be afraid, Joanna. We've come to take you from the island.'

The gunship settled on the lawn, the cabin door opened and Stephen and Valsa stepped out. Joanna looked at them for a few moments without speaking. Stephen had changed. He was no longer a crooked, broken creature, but stood with dignity, one arm about Valsa's waist and the other raised in welcome. Their joy in each other made Joanna's loss more painful, and suddenly she was sobbing. Valsa ran to her and cradled her in her arms.

28

Crispian Finds His Voice

The guns had been chattering all night. Benedict gazed across the city from the balcony of the parliament building and watched tracer fire lighting up the sky. A mortar shell exploded in the street below him, but he showed no fear. Crispian stood at his shoulder, his hands resting on the bullet-scarred parapet, and his eyes reflecting the flames of a burning house.

'We gambled and lost,' sighed Benedict. 'Two thirds of our troops are dead and the rest are so exhausted and demoralised they hardly have the will to fight on.'

'Better to die free men than live as Dimrat's slaves,' replied Crispian.

After his victory in the canyon, Benedict had marched his outlaw army to the capital and occupied it. The citizens had greeted them as heroes and celebrated in the streets, but their joy was short-lived. Legions of kilvarsts and nazdargs laid siege to the city and held it in a stranglehold. Food and medical supplies ran out, and the people died in thousands: each house a coffin, and the city, a giant morgue.

Benedict's troops had fought from street to street, but they were slowly crushed by Dimrat's forces. Now they only held the municipal square and few outlying buildings. The end was near.

Benedict turned and looked at his friend fondly. 'You're such a dreamer, Crispian. We soldiers are practical men. Some of us dream of power and glory, but our idealism is only as wide as the barrel of a gun. We may dress our trade in fine words and sentiments, but we are merely the mercenaries of death. Death is our trade. We kill to preserve life. That is the contradiction we must learn to live with.'

Crispian removed his hand from the parapet and placed it on his friend's shoulder. 'What are men and women without a dream? They are hollow people, hardly worthy of the title "human".'

Benedict's face was wistful. He envied Crispian's certainty and yet loved him for it. 'I often imagined this moment,' he reflected.

'What moment?'

'Forgive me! The moment of my death. I thought it would come unexpectedly, a bullet or a shell: a heroic end; a blaze of glory like a rocket exploding in coloured stars! But here I am waiting for death to arrive like an overdue train, and what am I

176

doing? I'm discussing moral questions with a fellow passenger.' Benedict laughed.

A burst of gunfire interrupted their conversation. A few scattered troops fled across the square, pursued by kilvarsts. Rumbling behind them came the tanks, their guns swivelling in grey turrets. The tanks drew up in formation outside the parliament building and the roar of their engines ceased.

Silence!

A ceremonial car drove slowly into the square and stopped in front of the tank divisions. A chauffeur opened the rear door and the president stepped out. Night was almost over and the grey sky began to brighten in the east.

The president looked up at the balcony and spoke. 'Crispian, Benedict—your defiance is futile. Surrender!'

'Never!' replied Benedict. 'If you want to gloat over me, Mr President, you will never have the satisfaction of gloating over a living man.'

'As you wish,' said the president.

There was a sharp retort from a sniper's rifle and Benedict staggered forward and tumbled over the parapet to the street below. The president strolled over to the sprawled body and nudged it with his foot.

'He's dead, Crispian! Your commander is dead. Surrender, or you'll join him on the cobbles,' the president mocked, but Crispian was not listening. The sun had climbed over the horizon and driven away the grey.

'Look!' cried Crispian. 'Dawn is breaking and the colours are returning to the land. Joanna's succeeded. We've won!'

The tank turrets opened and the death squad commandos clambered out and stared at the sky in disbelief. The grey drifted from the square like gun smoke and the city was drenched in colour. The president ran to and fro, commanding his troops to return to their tanks, but they ignored him and gazed towards the east. The doors of the parliament building were flung open and the outlaws dashed into the square, crying out in joy: 'The colours have returned to the land.'

Crispian, followed by Martha, Stephen and Valsa, ran to Benedict, but he was beyond help. Valsa closed his eyes with her fingertips and looked at Crispian. 'His task is over and yours begins. It is for you to build the new world.'

In the sight of all the people, Crispian wept over his friend. 'Where he fell, I will build a statue in his memory. As long as the land endures, he will be remembered.'

The president had attempted to escape from the square in his car, but it had been stopped by a mob. They beat against the windows and kicked at the door, howling at him like enraged animals. The chauffeur panicked and bolted, leaving the door ajar. Hands reached into the car and dragged the president out. His screams grew fainter, silenced by the dull, brutal thud of blows. When the mob scattered, he lay broken and dying, his blood trickling between the cobbles like the threads of a crimson web. A shadow passed over the square, dimming the sun. He opened his eyes and saw a huge airship floating above him.

Footsteps! Or was it the slow beat of his heart? He couldn't be sure. He tried to lift his head and look about him, but a terrible coldness gripped his limbs and he was unable to move. The footsteps stopped. The president opened his eyes and saw the Captain.

'You!' he spat, his voice hardly audible, and a trickle of blood bubbled from his lips and stained his shirt. The Captain looked down at the dying man, his eyes compassionate.

The president struggled to speak. 'Take your mercy and forgiveness away from me. I don't want them,' and he closed his heart against the appeal in the

Captain's eyes. The footsteps receded and the grey seized the president and bore him away.

*   *   *

Joanna sat behind Stephen and Valsa and watched the land unfold below her. The roar of the gunship's engine and the thunder of its blades made conversation difficult, but she already knew most of the story. The Captain had given Stephen and Valsa the co-ordinates of Dimrat's island and instructed them to rescue her.

'You can see the city now,' shouted Stephen. 'We'll arrive in about ten minutes.'

The city rushed to meet them, passing through all the stages of its history as they approached: a tiny hamlet of scattered houses barely visible against the skyline, growing to a village, and finally a city bristling with towers, spires, domes and skyscrapers. The gunship landed in the square and the three companions disembarked.

'It looks as if there's going to be a celebration tonight,' remarked Stephen, and he pointed to the stage that was being erected at the far end of the square. Pyramids of amplifiers rose from the cobbles and towered into the sky, and floodlights were suspended on pylons. Already the crowds were gathering in the square, a festive company of people who shared their scant food and greeted each other joyfully. Musicians tuned their instruments and rehearsed, provoking an outburst of cheering from the crowd.

'For a land where music and song were crimes, there seems to be no lack of talent. Where do they all come from?'

Valsa answered: 'They're from the airship. They're musicians in the Captain's band.'

The night was clear and warm, and beneath its ancient canopy the crowd grew, overflowing the square and the streets surrounding it. The atmosphere was electric, melting the crowd and forging it into one vast organism with a single soul and voice. The people awaited their troubadour, young and old together.

A deep silence fell on the crowd, a silence that gathered the dreams and hopes of the people and uttered them like a prayer.

Silence! And then a rocket whistled into the sky leaving a trail of fire in its wake. High above the crowd it exploded in a cluster of stars. A startled cry swept through the crowd and every face turned heavenwards. The night was torn apart with a sound like thunder. Galaxies of stars tumbled from the darkness and vanished, and worlds were born and died as if this night was the first of all creation. The fireworks painted living pictures on the canvas of the sky: forests of trees with trunks of flame and leaves of liquid gold shook their fruit into the night; gardens of flowers blossomed and then withered into darkness; unicorns, formed from white hot fire, raced across the sky, stars scattering from their beating hoofs like sparks; fish, scales glowing like rainbows, leaped from rivers of molten silver, and above them, butterflies with coloured wings danced on the breeze.

And then the night was dark and still again and the last echo of the fireworks died among the hills.

A single circle of light shone on the empty stage. A figure entered it and began to sing, the first notes drowned in a cheer that leaped from a million voices, soared skywards and shattered among the stars. The Captain was dressed simply in jeans and a white tee-shirt, but his presence and the power of his voice held the people captive. 'Joanna,' he called, after the first song ended, 'come and join me here.' Stephen and Valsa led the protesting girl through the crowd to the stage where the Captain waited. 'Come,' he said, beckoning to Joanna with his hand, 'you must sing with me.'

'I'm nervous and don't know what to sing,' she replied in a small, frightened voice.

'Sing the song you sang before the manageress,' he suggested, and his voice turned the key of Joanna's memory. She remembered the game of roulette and the bullet in the Captain's hand and she was no longer afraid. Bright-eyed and fearless, she stepped into the ring of light, hugged and kissed the Captain, and began to sing. Floodlights blazed on, first one battery and then another, until the stage was an island of light in a sea of upturned faces. The musicians sprang on stage, seized their instruments and accompanied her. At first Joanna sang alone, her voice husky and tuneful, and then the Captain sang the harmony, and suddenly a million voices joined her in the chorus:

> Death is conquered;
> Fear is vanquished.
> Dimrat's power
> At last is broken.

The crowd found its voice and banished Dimrat's last curse from the land.

When the song was over, Joanna slipped from the circle of light into a darkness haunted by Rumbold. She could hear the cheers and roar of applause, but the joy leaked from her and left her empty and sorrowful. Why couldn't he be here to share this moment? A lifetime seemed too long without him. Joanna was alone with her grief in a crowd that sang and danced with happiness.

The night was almost over when the Captain returned for his final encore. His voice was still strong and throbbed with power. 'I must go now, but before I do, I have one last task to fulfil: introduce your new president.' He turned and called Crispian and Martha and blessed them before the people. The crowd stood

181

and cheered, their applause rolling in wave after thunderous wave across the stage. Crispian clutched Martha's hand, frightened by the human sea that stretched before him.

Martha pressed her lips to her husband's ear and shouted above the welcome of the crowd: 'You were born for this, Crispian. The people await their president.'

Crispian stood silently before his people, unafraid. The crowd grew silent and waited expectantly. The words came as naturally as if they had been rehearsed: 'I have dreamed of this hour, but I cannot be your president.' A great cry of protest roared from the throat of the crowd. Crispian reached out his arms and silenced them. 'I cannot be your president unless you choose me. I have no wish for tyranny or power. What sort of leader would I be if, in this hour of liberty, I stole your freedom? Better people than me have laid down their lives for this day. If I were to take the name of president against your will, I would make their sacrifice meaningless. Let us not forget them, for our liberty was not purchased cheaply.'

Tears shone in Joanna's eyes as she remembered Rumbold. A hand touched her shoulder. 'Come, Joanna. It is time for you to leave.' It was the Captain.

She turned to Stephen and Valsa and asked: 'Aren't you coming?'

'No,' said Valsa, speaking for them both. 'We shall stay in this land and help Crispian rebuild it. The Captain has given me permission to remain.'

Joanna clung to them for a few moments. 'Goodbye,' she whispered. 'We will meet again.' And then she followed the Captain to his airship.

Joanna was going home.

29

The Journey Home

The airship sailed into the dawn, its prow rising to meet the rolling breakers of light that flooded from the east. The sight of the airship halted Crispian's words and he was silent. The vast crowd, following his example, turned their faces upwards and watched as the Captain departed.

Joanna stood in the ballroom and surveyed the land below her from a viewing window. The ballroom was deserted and the only sound was the muted throb of the engines and the creak of the ship as it floated across the sky. She embraced the silence and allowed it to caress her and bring order to her thoughts. Her adventures and the loss of Rumbold had shaken her neat and tidy world: destroyed it for ever. As she watched the land, she relived her experiences and tried to make sense of them. The loss of Rumbold opened a deep chasm of grief within her and she wept quietly. The woman struggled from her chrysalis and a new person was born: yet as Joanna watched her faint reflection in the airship's window, she was lost: a collage of impressions randomly glued about the name of Joanna Bradley.

Footsteps! They beat against the floor like drumbeats, growing louder as they converged on Joanna.

The girl stood and waited, recognising the rhythm of the Captain's steps. As he approached, his reflection filled the window and his eyes were wise and tender. He didn't say a word, but came to her and placed his arms about her shoulders as if she was a child in need of comfort. Joanna did not resist but snuggled up to him, reassured by his presence and the peace he lent to the silence. She was never sure how long he stayed with her, but it was not the length of time that mattered—it was the quality. He gave her the security to reassemble the fragments of her life and see herself again.

At last Joanna turned and spoke to the Captain. 'Why?' she asked, but there was no reprimand in her question, only pain and confusion.

The Captain grew tall and terrible and his face shone as brightly as a magnesium flare. Stars burst from his fingertips like blizzards of driving snow and in his palms she saw all worlds. 'Look,' he commanded, pointing at the airship's window, 'and you will understand.'

The window shone like a silver mirror, and reflected in it Joanna saw a company of giants. In their midst strode Rumbold. His face was young and joyful, and glory hung about him like a cloud.

'He is with his people in my country,' said the Captain. 'You weep for the loss of Rumbold, but he will never weep again. In your world he was an exile, but now he has found his true home. His journey is over; yours has just begun.'

Joanna was silent for a while. 'I've been very selfish,' she said, 'and have only thought of my own happiness.'

'It's human to mourn the loss of a friend, Joanna, but foolish to hold him when he's gone.'

Joanna breathed in the Captain's goodness like the smell of freshly baked bread. 'I've found it hard to trust you,' she said, 'but there's something else I've never told you: I love you! I loved you from the first moment you looked at me, but I didn't understand.'

'Thank you,' said the Captain simply, but his voice shook with joy. 'You're nearly home, Joanna. It is time for you to learn some of the secrets of my ship.'

'Secrets?' But before she could question him further, the view outside the window changed and she saw a planet ringed by five moons. The airship floated through the planet's atmosphere and plunged into a purple ocean. Joanna looked sideways at the Captain and screamed. He was no longer a man, but a spidery creature with waving tentacles and the multi-faceted eyes of an insect.

'Don't be afraid, Joanna. Look at the window.' His appearance was exotic, but his voice was the same, calming her fear.

Joanna obeyed. The airship hung above a plain covered in scarlet and yellow flowers. In the centre of the plain was a silver dome, and surrounding it were a number of hive-shaped dwellings. Joanna braced herself and looked at the Captain. He was a gnome, with a squat body, a huge eyeless head and an antenna rising out of his cranium like an aerial.

A succession of worlds appeared in the window and then vanished, and with each new world the Captain shed his human form and adopted the likeness of the creatures of that planet.

'My ship sails on many seas,' he explained, and his words awed Joanna with their majesty and truth. 'Even as we sail the skies of earth, we voyage across all worlds and exist in every place.'

The stars shone through the window of the airship, and below them twinkled the lights of a great city.

'You're home, Joanna. It's time for you to leave,' said the Captain, and he led her through the deserted ballroom, their footsteps ringing in the silence. The Captain knelt and opened the hatch, and a chill blast of wind blew into the airship. 'Goodbye, Joanna.' He took her hands in his and smiled, his eyes as tender as the autumn moon. 'You have given me joy, Joanna. You have done your job well and will always be my champion. Thank you for bringing the colour back to the land!' He kissed her and helped her onto the rope ladder.

Joanna climbed confidently down the flimsy ladder to her Brixton home. A gang of youths sauntered along the pavement towards her. 'Has your sugar-daddy brought you home in his airship?' snarled the leader of the pack, and he swaggered over to Joanna intent on mischief, or worse. His face was angular and brutal, and his hair was cropped short against his skull. He made a grab for Joanna, but she dodged him nimbly and left him clutching at air.

'If you want to kiss a girl, guy, ask her permission first,' advised Joanna reasonably. The gang jeered and goaded their leader.

He tried to grab her again, but she countered with a series of lightning blows that tumbled her attacker into the gutter. She turned to the gang and stared at them fearlessly. 'Hey guys, if his mummy asks what happened to him, tell her he was mugged by a sixteen-year-old girl.' And she opened the front door of her house, slipped inside and called out: 'Dad! Mum! I'm home!'

The Captain would be with her always and she was not afraid any more.

The Will Of Dargan

by Phil Allcock

Trouble has darkened the skies of the Realm: the Golden Sceptre crafted by the hands of Elsinoth the Mighty has been stolen. Courageous twins, Kess and Linnil, team up with an assorted company of elves and crafters—and set out to find it.

Their journey takes them through rugged mountains, gentle valleys and wild woods to the grim stronghold of Dargan the Bitter. Will they win back the Sceptre? The answer depends on their courage, friendship and trust.

Phoenix
Published by Kingsway

The Fading Realm

by Phil Allcock

The evil Dargan has recaptured the Golden Sceptre which is mysteriously bound up with the free will of the inhabitants of the Realm. As a result of his frightening new powers, parts of the Realm begin to fade, as Dargan seeks to subject all creatures to his twisted will.

Athennar, son of the Guardian of the Realm, leads his small group of friends towards a final confrontation with their dreaded enemy. Will their faith and courage be strong enough to resist Dargan's power? Or will the Sceptre become the unholy instrument of a new Lord of the Realm?

This is the dramatic climax to the story begun in *The Will of Dargan* and *In Search of the Golden Sceptre*.

Published by Kingsway

In Search Of The Golden Sceptre

by Phil Allcock

The evil Dargan has stolen not only the Golden
Sceptre but also Linnil, who is locked in an
underground cell. Kess and his friends set off across
the Realm once again to search for both Linnil and
the Sceptre.

Through clinging, dangerous mists to the northern
kingdom of the extraordinary Ice People, and the
beautiful but treacherous Jewelled Forest—they
struggle onwards. Only the love of Elsinoth and the
strength of their friendship can sustain them, but will
these be enough to thwart the devious plans of
Dargan?

Phil Allcock is also the author of *The Will of Dargan*, as well
as short stories for BBC TV.

Phoenix

Published by Kingsway

The Book And The Phoenix

by Cherith Baldry

Times are hard for most of the Six Worlds. Earth is
long forgotten, left behind in a past age when
technology brought men and women to the stars.

The old tales tell how, generations ago, the colonists
brought with them a belief, a faith, a way of life. But
that's almost forgotten now, just a dream for old men.

Until now. Young Cradoc will see a vision of the
legendary phoenix that will lead him to a Book. It is
only when he discovers the power in the Book that
he also learns there are many who will want to
destroy it—and anyone who attempts to protect it.

Published by Kingsway

Hostage Of The Sea

by Cherith Baldry

They came from over the sea, a nation of warriors intent on spreading their empire. When they descended upon a small kingdom that served the God of peace, the battle was short. And Aurion, the peaceful King's son, was the ideal hostage to secure victory.

Coming to the fearsome land of Tar-Askar, Aurion meets the strong and proud son of the warrior king. A most unlikely friendship develops—a bond of love that will prove a greater threat to the Tar-Askan empire than the weapons of war.

Also by **CHERITH BALDRY** in the *Stories of the Six Worlds: The Book and the Phoenix.*

Phoenix

Published by Kingsway